ELIZABE

Shadows of Doubt

PART FOUR OF THE LORING-ABBOTT SERIES

Cover Design by Wilette Youkey

Edited by Tessa Shapcott

ISBN-13: 978-0996575409

ISBN-10: 0996575405

For my Grandma Gwyndolen Lambert Davis, who showed me the world through an artist's eyes... and vacuumed in high heels.

ELIZABETH JOHNS

Shadows of Doubt

PART FOUR OF THE LORING-ABBOTT SERIES

Acknowledgements

Many thanks to:

Wilette. You are the reason people open my books in the first place.

Staci, Judy, Shae, Beth and Tina. I have come to rely on your opinions and support. Thank you.

Tessa. My editor, that makes me not dread that part of the process so much!

My family, for their continuous support and encouragement. Writing is not an 8 to 5 job.

Chapter One

Bloody Bath. How had he been reduced to this? He was stuck in dowager-debutante-invalid hell. Not that there was anything wrong with any of them in particular, but the amalgamation was daunting to a bachelor. There was nothing and no one else there—between the ages of twenty and sixty anyway.

And he wasn't *particularly* sought after: a mere mister, a Lord Nobody. Not that he was so meek to think his was not an attractive personage; only the few who'd turned his eye had loftier targets in mind. But, in fact, hardly any had turned his eye. Perhaps he had merely been too long with the Army; there was no doubt he had a courteous and cheerful disposition, but he enjoyed sparring with his bantering tongue, and few had the wits—or appreciation of humour—to match him long enough to maintain his interest.

He was certainly great for filling a dance card. He was a superb dancer and had exquisite taste in dress. And he was excellent at evening out the numbers. Mamas were not even afraid to leave their unwed daughters with him—he was too nice.

To make matters worse, his friends had succumbed to leg shackles. Every single one. Or, rather, they were not single any longer. He had to leave this Mecca for the unsingle-minded as soon as possible. If only he knew where to go.

France? No, as beautiful as it was, he had had enough of the Continent during his time with the Army, and recently, some French triplets.

London? No, he had already had his fill of society and matchmaking. He could only abide London in small doses.

A country house? The country was certainly appealing, but he would be bored within a fortnight by himself.

He looked out over the window from their townhouse on the Circus. There were children playing with their nannies and nurses pushing their new charges in prams around an older gentleman with his cane. He needed a change. A big change. He certainly could not remain in Bath much longer or his sanity would succumb.

His father, Sir Charles, had decided to settle here to be within a day's drive of both of his daughters and his grandchildren. His grandmother also showed a decided inclination for Bath, and both seem tickled to be within walking distance of the Upper Rooms, not that his grandmother would walk there. A night at the Assembly felt like the worst sort of punishment for Andrew. He was glad his father seemed content here, but he needed to move on.

It was difficult for an old soldier to settle down. He needed something meaningful with which to occupy his time. He did not wish to return to the Army of Occupation either. He had ended that chapter in his life, though Waterloo would always be with him, like it or not.

It must be his upcoming birthday causing his unrest. Thirty was not so old, yet he had no plan for the future. He must think of something, and soon. Melancholy was not his way and he felt it encroaching at an alarming pace.

"What has you in the dismals?" he heard his father, Sir Charles, ask from behind him.

"Am I so obvious?" He remained staring out the window with his hands in his pockets.

"You are hardly yourself these days. Are you bored?"

"I suppose. I am not certain what to do with myself now," Andrew said with a slight lift of the shoulders.

"Ah, I see."

He turned to look at his father, who had pinched his face in thought.

"And there is no one you wish to settle down with?"

Andrew shrugged again. "I need a holiday from marriageable misses. Apparently, I am not eligible enough in their opinions." Despite everyone's assumptions, he was not opposed to settling down, but had not yet found the proper person. Too many London Seasons had tended to lead him to cynicism about marriage.

"Why do you not enlighten them?"

He gave his father a look of mock abhorrence. "One doesn't blurt out 'I am as rich as Croesus' in the *ton*. Besides, I do not wish to be wanted solely for my property and my income."

"It is understandable, but it is also understandable for someone to desire security. Is that not what you would seek for your daughters?"

Andrew had not thought of it that way, but no one would ever be so openly vulgar. He shrugged. The wealth of the Abbotts was not well known; Sir Charles' vast estates were either let or in foreign holdings. Both men had been away for most of the decade, and were neither likely to boast or flaunt their wealth to anyone.

"What do you wish to do?" his father asked.

"That is the problem. I do not know."

He heard a loud sigh from his father. "I am loathe to bring this up, but it seems I have little choice. The plantation remains in need of much work after the fire. It seems that it is too much for Abe alone. I will be forced to sell if I cannot find someone I trust to rebuild and run it. I am getting on in years. I do not wish to return to America to live. Would you consider going to oversee the rebuilding and finding a proper steward?"

"I don't know, Father. America is rather distant. I thought I might attempt to settle down."

"Now that you're in your dotage? I do not wish for it to be permanent, Andrew. If you cannot find a trustworthy steward then I would ask you to sell the property after it is restored."

"I thought that was to be Elly's land. Should you not defer to her and Easton?"

"They have their hands full here. I would bequeath the earnings to her, of course."

Andrew pondered in silence.

"Something to consider. I will leave you to think on it."

Andrew needed to escape outside for a little while. He put on his beaver hat and began to stroll around. He would prefer a long hard ride, but Bath was not the ideal place with its steep hills. If he had not promised his grandmother to escort her to the Assembly tonight he would have headed out into the country. He shuddered. Another night charming old ladies and girls with spots.

~*~

Gwendolyn wanted to get away from Bath. She had lived near here her whole life but wanted to see the rest of the world. Desperately. She knew there was more to life, because she had read such things in books. But as long as her mother was ill, and she had no money, she would have to be content travelling through the written word. She fastened her bonnet and prepared to take advantage of this small reprieve. One of her mother's cousins and childhood playmates had moved to Bath and had been

10

calling for a few hours each day to sit with Mama, allowing Gwendolyn to have some fresh air. She pulled her bonnet down over her unruly mane and set out for her walk.

Mama became anxious when she was left alone. She had a servant in the house with her, but that was not the same. Thank goodness Mama was happy with her cousin. The time she had each day was a treasure. How had she maintained her sanity before?

She wandered around on the beautiful sunny day with little purpose, enjoying the taste of freedom. She walked down Milsom Street on her way to the circulating library and passed the colourmen's shop. She wished she could still afford to buy paints, brushes and canvas. Keep walking, she told herself. No point in letting her artist's genie out of the bottle, since she could not indulge it. She normally walked in a different direction so she would not allow herself to be tempted by things she could never have again. The dress shop next door held a celestial blue silk hanging in the window that she felt a pang of envy for.

She had long ago given up on having a London Season, or even one in Bath. She might have had a right to be there by her birth, but that was where the connection ended. The two times she had been to the Assembly, she had lurked in the shadows because she was insecure. She was never completely comfortable in large crowds—people tended to stare. She had also been forced to leave her school when her papa died. She knew most things properly, but had had little actual practice.

Still, it would have been nice to dress up like a princess and dance with a handsome prince. Once.

She had given up on those dreams becoming reality. Since Papa had died leaving them in penniless disgrace, and Mama needed her, any thoughts of her own situation were fruitless. She had missed the desirable age for marriage, and who would want to saddle themselves with a spinster and her ailing mother? She did not want to ponder how she would get by when her mama passed.

She entered the library and scanned the available works, all familiar and most nearly memorised. Burney, Edgeworth…

She heard the clock chime. Was it so late already? She would be obliged to run if she did not leave soon. She carefully selected her two allotted volumes. Even though the cost of a library subscription was dear, she had nothing else she would rather spend her money on. It was her escape from reality, her dreams fulfilled in another world.

She entered their rooms on Barnett Street breathlessly and tossed her bonnet on the table. She hoped she had made it before the Dowager left.

"Gwen, is that you?" she heard her mother's voice say quietly.

"Yes, Mama. Shall I bring in tea?"

"Not yet. Come in."

That was strange. Gwen walked into the parlour with a concerned look on her face. She curtsied to the Dowager and rushed over to her mother's side. She did not look well.

"Is something amiss?" she asked worriedly.

"No, my love. Cousin Henrietta has an invitation for you."

"Yes, your mother and I were discussing what is to be done with you. We have decided that you should accompany me to the Assembly tonight," the Dowager Duchess of Loring pronounced.

"That is extremely kind of you, Your Grace, but I could not." Gwen made meaningful eyes towards her invalid mother on the sofa. How could the Dowager think she could leave her mama?

"Your mother will be fine. We will only be a stone's throw away. I will send an extra servant here, who may fetch you should your mother need you. She will not be alone."

Gwen did not want to go. She was past the point of being marriageable and she was certainly too poor to attract any notice. If only she'd had such an offer before her world had come crashing down. She felt a twinge of guilt. She should not have been dreaming earlier...

"As grateful as I am for your offer, Your Grace, I no longer own anything suitable for the Assembly. Perhaps another time." She smiled gratefully. There would never be another time and she knew it.

Her mother lifted her head off of her pillow and looked directly at her. "Gwendolyn, I want you to go. I need you to go, for me."

She suffered momentary astonishment. Was this her mother speaking? Her mother fretted if she left the room for more than ten minutes. She looked back at the Dowager who nodded at her.

"Very well, Mother. If that is your wish."

The Dowager stood. "I must take my leave, Millicent. Gwendolyn, would you be as kind as to see me to the door?"

"Of course, Your Grace."

"I will send my maid over to help you dress. The carriage will be by for you at seven." She leaned in and said quietly, "Your mother is worried about what will become of you. Oblige her by appearing to enjoy yourself." She smiled knowingly at Gwen and walked out of the door.

~*~

He was being set up. And the worst part was, he knew it and his grandmother knew it, and she knew that he knew that she knew he knew. But he had already agreed to go beforehand, so he was stuck and she knew it. He did not mind meeting new people—a distant relation even— and he certainly did not mind helping out. Someone who was in need, as his gran had so painstakingly put it. However, he knew her motives were deeper than that. She had a look in her eye, a certain twinkle, when she was on a mission.

He had made a point of avoiding being the object of one of her missions until now. Unfortunately, he was the last man standing.

"Very well, Gran. Spill the truth. Is she four-score with warts, or is she sixteen with spots and eight chins?"

"Andrew Charles Abbott!"

He refused to feel guilty. He crossed his arms and stared.

His gran was nearly an octogenarian, and she had not reached that age without acquiring some skills.

"What is it you want from me? To smile at her? To dance with her twice? To bring her lemonade?"

"That all sounds lovely, yes." His grandmother nodded her satisfaction.

"And?" he prompted.

"That is all. Nothing more." She was silent, trying to look innocent.

"And?" He stopped his pacing and stared.

"Well, perhaps..."

"Aha! I knew it!"

"Young man, you forget yourself. You interrupted your grandmother. Now sit. You are irritating my delicate constitution."

He snorted. "As delicate as a..."

"Enough. I don't need any vulgar analogies. I was going to say some conversation would be nice. I know better than to attempt to force you in to anything."

He looked at her sceptically.

"Besides, she is a highly ineligible match, a penniless spinster. She missed her debut when her father died in disgrace, and has spent her bloom caring for her invalid mother, my cousin Millicent. I agreed to look after her if something should happen, to help her find an eligible position. She has little hope for anything more."

Andrew let out a whistle. His gran was serious. Now he pitied the poor girl. "I beg your pardon. I assumed you already had the wedding arranged in your mind."

"I?" She looked offended.

He knew it to be an act.

"Very well. I will try to show her a nice evening. If she is capable." Some ladies weren't.

"That's my boy. I knew you would understand."

He reached over and kissed her on the cheek. She patted his cheek in return. He was sure he was being manipulated somehow, but he just didn't know what he could do about it.

Hanson arrived and had trouble disguising her shock when she saw Gwen. Wild would not be the exact word Gwen would use to describe her hair, but when she considered the shade of red and the long curls that escaped her every effort to contain them, she supposed the description apt. She should be used to the stares after six-and-twenty years.

"Hello, Hanson. I see Her Grace did not warn you how much work I would be. You need not bother with my hair. It is impossible. No one has ever been able to tame it."

Hanson smiled and removed her mobcap.

Gwen burst out laughing. "I see you understand."

"Yes, miss. I can manage the hair. First, let us try the gown on. Mary here will make any alterations necessary, while I style your locks."

"Did you say gown?" Gwen turned to see another maid holding a dress bag and held it up when Hanson indicated. The two worked to remove the gown and hang it up for Gwen to view.

She looked to her old faded gown that she had planned to wear, six years out of fashion at least, and could not find words.

"It is one of her granddaughter's that she left here. Her coloring and size are similar. Should do nicely." Hanson knew her thoughts. It was as magnificent as the silk she had seen that day in Milson Street.

She stood in disbelief as the maids helped her into the gown and pinned the necessary adjustments for her frame. She almost looked beautiful again. She should pinch herself and wake up.

"This is a mistake." She shook her head back and forth.

"Pardon, miss?"

"I cannot go. There is no point. Why pretend?"

"Miss, you'll pardon my saying so, but what's the harm?"

"A taste of something I will never have again is the harm."

"I see ye like books." The maid indicated the stack Gwen had just brought from the library.

Gwen nodded wondering what Hanson was alluding to.

"Pretend yer the heroine of a book. Dance with yer handsome prince."

"As if one would dance with me." She shook her head. "I am sorry. Self-pity is unbecoming at best."

She saw the maid's point, but this was different. There would be real people with whom she would have to interact, people who were not comfortable socially with someone who had lost everything. The poor widow and spinster daughter. And her looks. If she was rich and titled, people would call her exotic.

"Her grace thought ye might try to change her mind, and said to remind ye of yer mother."

Gwen sighed. Her mama had been adamant, which was strange.

16

"Oh, very well." It might be her last chance.

She stepped out of the gown, and Mary went to work on it.

"Now for your hair." Gwen tried not to get her hopes up. She had never had her own maid to dress her hair. She had not had her locks cut in years. She unwound the untidy knot and her hair fell down her back in riots of curls.

She expected the silence. Hanson finally broke it.

"Mary, if you would please go fetch me some scissors and pomade. And oil."

"Oil?" Gwen questioned in fear.

"Aye, miss. We are going to need everything we can find."

One hour, two feet cut off, and a bottle of hair oil later, Hanson let out a gasp of pleasure at her handiwork.

"Oh, miss! Do you have a glass you can look in?"

"My mother has a small one in her dresser."

"We have no time for that, miss," Mary reminded. "The carriage will be here to pick you up soon."

The maids helped her into the gown, and she hurried downstairs to meet the carriage.

She stopped to check on her mother.

"Oh, Gwen!" Her mother burst into tears. Well, going to the Assembly had been a nice thought. She should have known her mother could never go through with it.

"It is all right, Mama," she said in resignation. She bent over to comfort her. "I will not leave you." She resigned herself to staying home after all and began to sit down.

"No! You will wrinkle your gown. I am only crying because of how beautiful you look. I have taken your life away from you."

17

"No, Mama. Father did that."

Through her mother's weeping she did not hear the carriage roll up.

"I beg your pardon, miss," Hanson spoke up. "The carriage is here to fetch you."

"Go! Do not worry about me," her mother insisted bravely, while clutching her handkerchief.

Gwen looked at her weak and weeping mother hesitantly but nodded, kissed her on the cheek, and went to the door. She nearly fell as the door opened upon her.

"Oh!"

Two large hands steadied her.

A deep voice said, "I beg your pardon, miss."

She looked upward into a set of stunning blue eyes. She was speechless.

Apparently, so was he.

She heard a throat being cleared from the carriage.

"Miss Lambert, this is my grandson, Major Andrew Abbott."

~*~

This was the poor old penniless spinster? His gran must have been playing a joke on him. He snapped his jaw shut. He hadn't realised he had left it gaping open. He would play along for tonight. He escorted her to the carriage. He sat across from the girl and tried not to stare. He had never seen anything like her. She did not look old or penniless. He braved a sideways glance at his grandmother and saw a satisfied grin across her face. He would really like to stick his tongue out and make a face at her. Yes, he felt like a greenhorn youth sitting across from this vision in the carriage.

"I like what Hanson did with your hair, Gwendolyn."

"Thank you, Your Grace."

"You should not Your Grace me, Gwendolyn."

"I forget."

Gwendolyn. That was a fitting name. She was blushing. Then she smiled. She had dimples. He had a weakness for dimples. And red hair. This was going to be a long night.

He would be fortunate to be able to even secure her for two dances. Females who looked like her were not wallflowers, though she did appear to be shy as he noticed her looking at her hands or out the window instead of making eye contact.

He was intrigued, but he was leaving at the end of the week, so he would just have to remain so.

Chapter Two

The Upper Assembly Rooms already held a great crush by the time they arrived. Mr Abbott was escorting his grandmother and Gwen fell in behind. The elders had already retreated to the card room, and the youth were dancing exuberantly in the ballroom. The master of ceremonies greeted the Dowager with all the pomp and condescension he felt to be her due. When he came to Gwen, he repeated her name with a hint of recognition and a flash of distaste in his eyes. Of course, he knew who she was, and of her unfortunate circumstances, it was his business to know. However, he did not insult her openly since she was with such an exalted *parté*.

The Dowager made her way into the room, greeting old acquaintances as she went, and scanned around for a place that would give her the most advantageous view.

Gwendolyn tried her best to ignore the stares, but she felt them like a searing heat permeating her to the core. Her face heated, despite her fervent wish to remain indifferent. She did not want to be noticed or let them know they affected her so. She had hoped the memory of the old quizzes would be failing, but that was not the way Bath worked. It was well known a long memory was required to be one of the notorious nags. But would they dare shun her under the protection of the Dowager Duchess?

"This will do nicely," the Dowager said with approval as she selected a high bench to hold court.

Gwen tried not to panic when the Dowager chose a spot in full view of the crowd. She automatically began looking for a potted plant for refuge.

Mr Abbott was still nearby—too nearby for her comfort. He had watched her during the extravagantly short carriage ride to the Rooms with the same look most men gave her when they first saw her. She had immediately averted her eyes from the unwanted attention.

He was a fashionable London gentleman, and she was instantly aware of an attraction to him, which set up her guard. She hoped he would retreat to the card room. She wanted the fewest witnesses possible to view her discomfort. He no doubt knew of her penury from her living situation, but it was unlikely he knew the circumstances of her family's fall. Most town bucks seemed to assume she was available for a left-handed marriage when they found her penniless and her name disgraced.

"Go along, you two." The Dowager made a shooing motion with her hand, and Gwendolyn looked about to see if she was speaking to her or someone else. Mr Abbott stood there with a handsome smile and held out his arm to her.

"Shall we, Miss Lambert?" He offered his arm gallantly.

"Shall we what, Mr Abbott?" She looked at his arm as if it had the plague.

"Why, dance of course." His face took on a look of perplexity.

"Must we?" she whispered and began to panic.

"Yes Gwendolyn, you must. I insist. I brought you here to enjoy yourself," the Dowager said with finality. "Your name was added for the next dance, my dear."

She most definitely would have stayed at home had she known that. The Dowager had mentioned nothing about her handsome grandson's attendance or dancing. It was as far from an evening's enjoyment as she could imagine. She had convinced herself of having no acquaintance or consequence; she was certain she would be assured some measure of anonymity. Mr Abbott wound his arm through hers and patted her hand reassuringly.

"Come now, it will not be so bad. And better yet, it will make her cease her prattling." He winked at his grandmother as he said this.

"You do not understand, sir. I have had very little experience with dancing in years. I might be able to fudge my way through a country dance, but a quadrille…" She was trying to will her trembling to stop. Her previous encounters with such estimable gentlemen from London several years ago had left her without confidence.

"Ah, I see. That matters not. No one will notice your mistakes I assure you, for they will be too busy watching my clumsiness. However, I enjoy myself immensely so I pretend I know what I am doing and smile. There is no need to fret, I assure you."

They were already in formation, the set about to begin; it was too late for objections, though her insides were churning with fear. The square formed and the music began.

"Tell me, Miss Lambert, how I have never before had the pleasure of making your acquaintance?"

"I do not go about in Society. Certainly not in London."

She was uncomfortable making eye contact with one such as he, a London swell by the appearance of him… but it was difficult not to look. Her eyes were drawn to him inexplicably. Or not so inexplicably. She took the opportunity to survey him as he took a turn with a different partner in the figure. The exquisite cut of his superfine coat highlighted his broad shoulders, and snug satin breeches left little doubt as to the status of his athletic physique. The intricately folded cravat identified him as a dandy, but the becoming natural way he allowed his locks to fall and the understated neatness of his dress belied the appearance of

22

sense over the current fashions. Bath was certainly not often graced with specimens of his ilk.

She swallowed. "I gather, sir, that you have not spent much time in Bath," she commented. She began a turn with her next partner before rejoining him in the dance.

"You are correct. This is my first long visit," he responded when rejoined with her.

"Lucky fellow, indeed. For I have never been anywhere beyond the Bath countryside, much though I may wish to."

"Never been out of Bath? I should go mad," he said with dramatic shudder.

"Perhaps I am a bit mad," she said thoughtfully with a slight smile.

"Indeed?" His blue eyes twinkled, and her insides did a flip. She should not have made eye contact.

"Were it not for your grandmother, I would be. Her presence has allowed me some daily reprieve."

"That brings up a most important question. Where does one find sport or exercise here? Everywhere I look, save a few small parks, there are stone buildings, stone paths, stone churches. I am desperate for a ride or walk and there are none to be found. I *need* some nature, Miss Lambert," he said in a serious tone that was undermined by the crinkles around his eyes.

"Parading around the Pump Room constitutes exercise in this city," she said with mild sarcasm.

"Indeed. I've had the pleasure of strutting my feathers at that exalted establishment. However, if that putrid water does anything more than cause indigestion, I would happily eat my cravat!" he exclaimed with a serious face.

"Sacrilege! You will find yourself cast out of the town," she said with twitching lips. She agreed wholeheartedly, but people flocked to Bath for its healing waters. "You are not one for city life?"

"I have spent time in town, of course, but never for long. Ten years in the Army has taken me many places, but rarely to cities."

He led her through the dance, covering her mistakes with practiced grace. She had remembered most of the steps by her next change. He had made her feel at ease, such that she did not realise the dance had ended when he held out his arm to her.

"Thank you, Miss Lambert. I do not think anyone even noticed any of my missteps."

"You know very well it was quite the opposite." She smiled despite herself and fanned herself more furiously than proper due to the suffocating heat. She was grateful Hanson had thought to bring her one that matched her toilette.

"I know no such thing except it is a dashed crush in here. Shall we fetch a lemonade?"

A glass of lemonade was procured from the tea room, and they made their way to the small courtyard just beyond the door to the ballroom. They remained within view of the door for propriety, though many couples had sought relief out of doors.

"You mentioned the Army. Were you involved in the Peninsular Campaign? Or did you go to the American War?"

"I stayed on the Continent. Mostly as a part of Wellington's staff."

"I am most envious, sir. The Continent sounds very beautiful in many places, especially Italy and Greece."

"You have heard correctly. There is no place quite like them. The waters are the most incredible shades of blue. Nothing at all like the dark seas around England."

"You are most fortunate to have seen them, Mr Abbott. I've never even seen the English seas. I long to see the world—or at least see beyond the Bath countryside."

"I've also been obliged to see and stay in some locales revolting enough to make your skin crawl. Why have you not travelled?"

She ignored his question and changed the subject. She did not wish to go into depth over her situation, less he pity her. He likely had enough inclination from his grandmother about her status. Perhaps a fashionable town man like him thought he was doing her a favour by paying her marked attention.

"There are some nice walks and rides nearby. I shall be happy to give you direction."

"You are most generous. Would you be so obliging as to show me one of them tomorrow?"

"I am afraid I cannot leave my mother for so long, sir. I have not been to the Assembly in nearly six years." She had neither time nor luxury to indulge this fancy.

"Six years?" He nearly spewed his lemonade.

"Until your grandmother began visiting daily, I rarely left her at all."

"I am certain something could be arranged."

She shook her head. "No, sir. I thank you kindly for the offer, but it is not possible."

She set down her glass and began walking towards the Dowager. She had to put a stop to this immediately.

~*~

He watched Miss Lambert walk off in a glorious gown of satin that seemed designed exclusively for her. If he hadn't seen his sister Elly wear the gown before he never would have known it was a hand-me-down. However, he hadn't noticed his sister's long legs or how the fabric had clung to her curves when she'd worn it. He could not seem to force his eyes to look away, the fool he was, before he recalled himself to escort Miss Lambert and follow along.

She was enchanting. She had none of the practiced charms or coquettishness of the females in town, and he found he had no idea how to behave with her. She was without affectations and completely unaware of her attractions. It was a very good thing he was leaving for America this week—or was it? Would it be so terrible a match? Likely. He would fall for her head first and she would tolerate him out of gratefulness.

He had nearly sworn off females after the Ashbury triplets. He had enjoyed their company, but the spark he desired had been missing. He was not hindered in his search as so many were by the pressing need for an heir. No, he had nieces and nephews in abundance to leave his property to. He could not blame the triplets entirely, and at least his heart was not injured, only his pride. Their hearts belonged to other men, and he did not want anyone at that cost. They had used him much the same as he had used them in return—as flirtatious friends and beautiful companions.

After she was returned to his grandmother, he watched Miss Lambert for some time from across the room, waiting until it was proper to ask her to dance again. He conversed with the elder veterans, many retired here with their injuries, all eager to reminisce about their Army or Navy days, and hear retold the stories of the now infamous battles of Waterloo and Trafalgar.

Several young men approached the Dowager, hovering nearby, hoping for an introduction, but Miss Lambert subtly shook her head or whispered to his grandmother. Why wasn't his grandmother introducing her and insisting she dance? And what did she mean by trying to pass herself off as a spinster? He could feel the piercing looks from his grandmother from across the room. He raised a questioning eyebrow at her. Did she expect him to break the rules for Miss Lambert? That would only draw unwanted attention to her.

He noticed the forlorn look on one of Miss Lambert's admirers as he walked away.

"What happened old fellow? The beauty isn't dancing anymore tonight?"

"Apparently not."

"Perhaps she was overly fatigued or concerned to leave her companion."

"Her Grace said hello, and asked after my family, but did not perform the introduction."

"Did you ask her to be introduced?"

"No. It did not seem welcome for she changed the subject every time I began to ask! One does not interrupt Her Grace!"

"No, indeed. Who can say with those on the verge of senility? Perhaps the Dowager did not realise your intent. I suppose I must rescue the damsel from the Dowager's grasp."

"I'll bet you a monkey she won't dance with you again," he said defensively, not wanting his own confidence demeaned further.

"Save your monkey and learn from the master." Andrew winked at the young pup.

He casually made his way back to Miss Lambert's side and offered his hand to her for their second dance. He saw her hesitation. She wanted to refuse him. Sadly for her, he was not here to be refused.

"You cannot deny me as you have done the others, for I have been introduced. It would be badly done," he said, unperturbed.

She sighed. "If you insist, Mr Abbott."

"The sentiments I long to hear from all of my partners," he said cheerfully.

"You have been most attentive this evening. I shall inform your grandmother of your good behaviour." Her eyes danced as she took his arm and let him lead her to the set.

"I am not dancing attendance on you at her behest, thank you."

"Are you not?" she asked with a sceptical eyebrow.

"Not completely." He grinned at her, unashamed. "Now tell me what worries you so? Are you not enjoying yourself?"

"Am I so obvious? I apologise. I did not mean to be ungrateful." She wrinkled her brow.

"Only to me. I am used to giddy, chatty females at balls." Or widows who wanted something else entirely. "You are different."

"I warned you I do not attend social functions anymore, sir. I have no place in Society any longer. I am unpracticed in polite conversation, though I will try to behave better. I promised I would try to enjoy myself."

"Do you not enjoy dancing? I assure you your skills are equal to that of most present."

"I suppose I like it well enough, but to make small talk with strangers that I shall never see again is beyond the effort required to make it enjoyable," she said while attempting to suppress a grin.

"So severe, Miss Lambert," he teased. "Could you not pretend to be hard of hearing and ignore their questions?"

"I find it easier to avoid the introduction in the first place."

"Indeed." His eyes twinkled in appreciation. "Now what truly troubles you?"

She sighed. "I'm worried about my mother. I confess it is hard not to be concerned."

"I can escort you home if you wish, Miss Lambert."

"No," she shook her head. "It is not necessary."

"I know the assemblies in the fast town of Bath last until eleven of an evening, you know. Quite scandalous. I even heard the Lower Rooms go until midnight."

She laughed. "Mr Abbott, are you ever serious?"

"Only when duty requires it. There now, a beautiful smile. I had to work very hard for that one." He gave her a meaningful look. He escorted her back to his grandmother when the dance had finished.

"I find I am quite fatigued, ma'am. Miss Lambert's dancing prowess has taxed me greatly. Would it be bothersome to you if we leave early?"

The Dowager looked to Miss Lambert knowingly. "Your mother is fine, dear. But we may go. You have had your dances and some lemonade, so I am satisfied."

Andrew scoffed within earshot of his grandmother, and she ignored it.

The carriage was brought around and they dropped Miss Lambert at her rooms.

"I will call for you at the usual time tomorrow, Gwen. Perhaps you can show my grandson about Bath tomorrow."

Miss Lambert opened her mouth to protest, but held it back and said instead, "Thank you for the lovely time tonight, Ma'am. Mr Abbott." She gave a small curtsy and he escorted her to her door. "Goodnight, Miss Lambert."

"Goodnight, Mr Abbott."

~*~

Gwen let herself quietly in the door in an attempt to not wake her mother. But when she walked through the parlour, her mother was on the sofa waiting for her.

"Mama! Why did you wait up for me? You must be exhausted," Gwen exclaimed. "And where are the Dowager's servants?"

"I sent them away. I was too excited to see how the ball went to sleep." She made an effort to sit upright and patted the spot next to her. "Please come tell me all about it. I'm sure you were the hit of the evening."

"Oh, Mama. It was all right. Duchess Loring's grandson escorted us."

"Mr Abbott? I thought I heard a man's voice earlier. Was it he who picked you up dear?"

"Yes, Mama." She tried to fidget with her dress so her mother did not see her blush. It was ridiculous to even think about Mr Abbott in such a way.

"He is handsome then? I have not seen him since he was a boy."

"Yes, Mama. He is very handsome. But not for the likes of me."

"Why ever not Gwendolyn? You are of equal birth."

"Equal birth, perhaps. But not equal standing. I have little to offer but a tarnished name and poverty."

"Did he treat you with disdain?" she asked, horrified at the thought.

"No, Mama." She shook her head in adamant denial. "He was everything wonderful, I assure you. He almost made me forget my circumstances. He danced with me twice, he procured lemonade for me, and conversed with me—he was everything delightful."

"Then whatever is the matter?"

"Nothing is the matter, Mama." She reached over and took her mother's hand and gave her a reassuring smile. "The evening was perfect. Do not put your hopes in that quarter, however, I beg of you. Mr Abbott will not be long in Bath. He has no thoughts of marriage, I am certain."

"Gwendolyn, I never meant to hold you back." Her mother looked down as tears began streaming from her eyes. She tried to blot them away with a shaky hand. "You've had to waste away your bloom caring and devoting yourself to your invalid mother."

Gwen scooped her fragile mother into an embrace but both ladies could not help but succumb to a bout of tears.

"You are not holding me back, Mama. The thought never occurred to me. But hoping for a brilliant match with him is unreasonable. He is likely diverting himself with little else to do in Bath—and perhaps doing a favour for his grandmother."

"I refuse to stop hoping for your future, Gwendolyn. Whatever will become of you? I am growing weaker by the day. I cannot control these shakes and I cannot seem to balance properly to walk without falling."

"Please do not speak so! I will be fine when that day comes, a long, long time from now. I am content with my situation." At least she had been until tonight.

"Gwen, there is your father's family, should you become desperate. Cousin Henrietta informed me that your uncle died some time ago and your cousin Peregrine is the new viscount. He might be willing to help you."

"I will not beg to a family that made certain they repudiated us! If the new viscount, my *cousin* Peregrine, were so amiable, he has had ample time to make up for the destitution we were left in when my father and brother died. No, I would rather make a living on my back than crawl to him for help."

"Gwendolyn!" her mother reproached.

"He and James were the best of friends were they not, Mother? He may be more pleasant than his father, but one does not abandon one's family or best friend when in trouble if you are of noble character! Please do not speak of it."

"But there was something you were to have known, if I could recall," her mother said hesitantly.

"No. I beg of you, do not exert the effort. I do not want to know. Come now. Let us get you to bed, you must be fagged."

"Now that I know you are home, perhaps I may sleep."

She saw her mother into her bed and kissed her good night.

"Gwen, I am glad you went even if you do not think it useful, I do."

"Then I am happy I went."

"One day you will find a man that cares not for fortune. Beauty and a kind heart can cause a man to overlook other unfortunate circumstances that were none of your doing."

"Pray, hope that you are correct."

"Sweet dreams, love."

She smiled and blew out the taper. She knew she would dream all right, but bittersweet was more like it.

~*~

"It is an utter disgrace. Shameful! And the coward isn't here to witness the suffering he caused," the Dowager exclaimed as soon as the carriage door was closed.

"What happened precisely?" Andrew asked curiously.

"Gambling. Her father lost every penny and then some. Fortunately, a commission had already been purchased for the son."

32

"Or not so fortunately," Andrew reflected from personal experience.

"Quite so, dear."

"And what became of the father? One does not die of disgrace or the world would be a more pleasurable place entirely."

"After is where the true scandal happened. He called the partner a cheat and was summarily dispensed with at ten paces by one of Manton's finest."

Andrew whistled understanding.

"I believe once the initial disgrace passed, Cousin Millicent was so ill she could not leave the house."

"From what does Mrs Lambert suffer?"

"You know, I am not entirely sure. It would not be polite to ask, and Millicent will not speak of her troubles even to me."

"That is very unlike most females of delicate constitution that I know," he added with his usual flare of sarcasm.

His grandmother swatted him with her fan.

"What will happen to her?" he asked in a more serious tone.

"To Gwendolyn?"

"And Mrs Lambert, should she survive."

"They survive on percentages from our grandmother's estate, but it will cease to exist when she does."

"And Miss Lambert will have nothing." Andrew could spit. He wanted to crawl through hell and make the selfish, greedy, snake suffer more than Hades himself.

"Indeed."

"And her Lambert side of the family?"

"Cast them off. The old Viscount Kendall was a pompous prig. To put it mildly."

"Kendall? His son seems a tolerable fellow. A bit too foppish for my tastes, but decent nevertheless."

"He has made no efforts to repair the connection to my knowledge."

"He likely has not thought of it. And she received no offers?"

"After her father's fall from grace, the only offers she received were not honourable ones."

Andrew made a disgusted noise.

"She is intriguing and beautiful. But with no fortune, she has little hope to form an eligible alliance."

"Unfortunately, I am familiar with how most men would view her station," he said, with growing trepidation. "What do you mean to do? Or more specifically, what do you mean for me to do?"

"You do not have to do anything, dear. But you want to. And what is the harm? You leave soon."

Andrew was thinking a great deal of harm could occur in a few days. He should run away as fast as he could. It was unlike his grandmother to encourage him to dangle after an unmarried lady for mere friendship.

"I only wish to see Gwendolyn enjoy herself. No one should be stuck inside those dreary rooms for the better of six years."

"Definitely not. I am going mad being in Bath for six days."

"Then I shall take care of cousin Millicent while you take care of Gwendolyn."

Yes, he should most certainly run. But his feet did not seem to be cooperating.

Chapter Three

The next day, Gwen tried to forget about Mr Abbott. She would not be
attending any more balls, and would certainly not be traipsing about the
countryside with him as if she had not a care in the world, as if she were
a naïve debutante and still an eligible match for the likes of him. He had
not treated her with any disrespect, but that did not mean he intended
anything honourable. He had nothing else to gain from acquaintance
with her, and she would do very well to remember it.

Why the Dowager had taken it into her head to thrust Gwen back into
society, when she had no hope for a grand match with a less than
illustrious family background, was beyond provoking. The Dowager did
not like to take no for an answer, but she would have to. Gwen would not
be her pet project. They would leave town and she would have to face
the gossip again. The recollection still hurt six years later.

The Dowager arrived like clockwork at precisely two in the afternoon.
She brought Mr Abbott with her, as promised. Gwen steeled herself for
the conversation to come. Her mother had dressed with unusual care,
thrilled at the prospect of Mr Abbott's visit. She was very tired, however,
from the exertion and sat upright in the parlour with difficulty.

Greetings and formal introductions made, the Dowager made herself
comfortable. Mr Abbott remained standing looking about the room,
handsome as sin with his unaffected manners.

"That is a lovely painting. It isn't quite right for a Delacroix or
Gainsborough though," he was studying the painting on the wall with
great interest.

"I'm afraid not, Mr Abbott. All such luxuries have long been sold,"

Gwendolyn remarked.

"You view the talents of my Gwendolyn, here," her mother replied.

"Upon my word, Miss Lambert! You painted this?" Mr Abbott said with astonishment.

Gwen's mother beamed with pride, while a flush began to creep over Gwen. She did not know how to accept praise. She'd had no practice.

"I used to paint as a hobby. I once fancied myself a future master." She raised her eyebrow to show her self-mockery.

"You are too modest. I would venture to disagree, but can see you will hear none of it."

"You are correct, Mr Abbott. I do not paint any longer."

"Where was this landscape made?" he refused to move on from the painting.

"You may see the poor imitation of the landscape for yourself if it is exercise you want, Mr Abbott. The walk boasts an incredible view."

"Just when I had resolved to take the waters at the Pump Room," he quipped.

She gave him a look. While appreciative of his sentiments, she must remain impervious to his charm. "I have written out directions for several activities for you to embark upon during your time here." She held out a piece of paper containing a list of a dozen ways he could spend his idle time.

"Why do you not show Andrew the view yourself, Gwendolyn? You do not need to go to the lending library every day, dear," the Dowager suggested.

Of course she did. That was how she survived. She hesitated on how to answer tactfully.

"I will not accept no for an answer, Miss Lambert. Besides, it is my birthday and it is my wish," Mr Abbott said charmingly.

"Your birthday? Why should you wish to spend it with me?"

"Why not?" He was holding his arm out for her and smiling. He was handsome. Devastatingly so. Her mind was protesting loudly, but her heart was screaming yes! She looked towards her mother, who was smiling and nodding encouragement. She would not win this round with three against one. She headed towards the door in resignation.

"Very well. I must warn you, it will be brisk to return in time." She donned her bonnet and tied the strings as he held the door for her.

"In time for what?" He looked behind them. "Don't you need a maid?"

"I am too old and too poor to be concerned with a chaperone, sir."

He stared at her in confusion.

"Your grandmother generously comes by every afternoon so that I may have some time. I must return by the time she leaves."

"I see. And you have no one that can stay with her?"

"No. Until the Dowager began visiting, there was no one else Mama was comfortable with."

"If you will beg my pardon for asking, what ailment does your mother suffer from?"

"Primarily, an affliction of the nerves. But, she also suffers severe anxieties."

"Then let us move with purpose. I am very empathetic to anxious nerves."

"I do not mean to do her an injustice. She does not suffer nervous spasms as I have seen in many females with a bent towards the dramatic."

"Is there anything to be done?"

"I fear not. Mr Norman, the apothecary, seems to think it a disorder tied to her mind, for she becomes addled when she has an attack. Not only do her wits suffer, but her breathing, and her body trembles insufferably." She shook her head in self-reprimand. "Forgive me, I do not know why I am rattling on like a chatterbox."

"Do not trouble yourself, Miss Lambert. I have often been told I am a good listener. Your confidences shall go no further."

"You are very kind. I suppose with no one else to talk to for six years, I suddenly feel the need to blurt out all of my worries at the first sympathetic ear. How vexatious of me!"

"Not at all. It is a relief from the usual female jibbering on about bonnets, slippers and gowns. Although, in my youngest sister's defence, she is not concerned in the least with fashion."

"How many sisters do you have, Mr Abbott?"

"Two. Lady Abernathy and Lady Easton. Do you have any siblings? I think I heard you had a brother in the Army."

"I had a brother, but he fell in the Peninsular Campaign." She looked away to blink back tears. His loss never stopped hurting.

"Please accept my condolences."

"Thank you, Mr Abbott. Or should I call you Major? You were also many years in the Army, I believe your grandmother said."

"I answer to either. And many other names," he chuckled. "I do not believe your brother and I were acquainted. Was he a hussar?"

"No, he was infantry. A captain in the Light Division."

"The 95th or 52nd?"

"The Light Bobs."

"Ah, under Colburne."

"I believe so."

A comfortable silence fell between them, and they were both breathing

38

heavily with exertion by the time they reached the pinnacle of the Beechen Cliff walk overlooking the Avon Valley. They took in the beauty in silent appreciation. The River Avon snaked through the town, and the sun highlighted the city made of golden stone.

"You captured the likeness very well." He surveyed the scene with approval.

"Thank you, sir. You could hardly say else."

"I could have said nothing at all, merely remarked on the lovely view. I do believe I prefer your version, however. You added in the elms here and the cliffs there, did you not?" he indicated with his hands where the additions had been made.

"You are very observant, Mr Abbott."

"Much good it does me. Though it often makes one more aware of beauty, it also has the opposite effect."

"Indeed."

"But, I feel much better about leaving Bath now that I know it affords such a vista."

"Leaving? So soon?" she felt a pang of sadness despite her minute acquaintance.

"I'm afraid duty calls me to America."

"America? You return to the Army, then?"

"No, familial duty."

"You have family there?"

"No," he held out his arm to lead her back down the path. He pulled an orange from his pocket and began to peel it as they walked slowly down the steep hill. "My father was the minister there before and after the war began. We still own a plantation there that was burned when the war came ashore."

He handed her half of the orange, which she took hesitantly and bit into a slice of heaven.

"The house remains in need of repairs and a steward to run it. We have a capable man for the farming at least."

"Have you been to America before?"

"I visited once before, in the small window of reprieve from Napoleon."

"Which part of America?" she asked eagerly.

"Just outside of Washington, near Virginia. The plantation borders the eastern coast of America, so it is a fairly easy trip. I do not have to bushwhack my way across the frontier, or forage through the wilderness."

She laughed and almost hit his arm reprovingly in jest, but stopped herself before she did something so familiar. It was for the best this man was leaving. She was beginning to feel dangerously attracted to him and his easy ways.

"I would love to see America one day," she said longingly.

"Perhaps you shall." He turned and looked at her. Their eyes met and she trembled slightly with anticipation. For what, she knew not. He swallowed and continued, "But today, we shall see more of Bath." He began walking again. "Is there anywhere to procure an ice in Bath?

By the time they made it back down the path into the town, dark clouds were forming and the wind was beginning to howl.

"Are you sure you want an ice, Mr Abbott?" she asked doubtfully.

"At this point, I will be happy to escape a soaking. Do you know anywhere we may take shelter quickly?"

Her bonnet blew off and she barely caught it. But when Mr Abbott looked at her, with a look she could not name, his mouth was gaping at her riot of curls tumbling about her. She had done her best with it that morning, but having had to wash the oil out from the ball meant it was at its wildest. She had no team of maids to dress her hair every day. She hastily tried to re-pin it and nodded towards the nearest shop she was certain of welcome. Mr Abbott led her into the colourist's shop, where she used to spend hours carefully selecting canvas, brushes and colour. It would be torture being there, seeing the pity on old Mr Scott's face. Were it only herself, she would have rather braved the storm and returned home.

~*~

"Miss Lambert, is that you?" The hair always gave her away. She turned to see Mr Scott, her old friend and painting teacher, was now an old man.

"Mr Scott, it is I. How are you?" She held out her hands and greeted him.

"It has been too long, my dear." His face filled with sadness.

"It has." They need not speak about why, for they both knew.

Remembering Mr Abbott's presence, "Forgive me. I was trapped in nostalgia. May I present my friend, Mr Abbott—Mr Scott."

"A pleasure." Mr Abbott made a courteous bow. "It is a shame Miss Lambert has given up painting. Her talent is rare."

"Aye. Many people fancy themselves masters, but hers is real talent. I still keep some of her work in my studio."

"You do?" She could not remember any of her works that would be worth keeping that had not already been sold.

"May I see?" Mr Abbott asked eagerly.

"Of course, right this way."

There in his own studio, where he taught lessons on occasion, were two of her early works. One, a still life, the other was of a horse grazing in a pasture.

"Those were my first paintings," she exclaimed as she walked over to them.

"Yes, but you showed great promise even then. I use them to instruct my current pupils."

"They are lovely, but I confess the landscape to be my favourite," Mr Abbott said thoughtfully as he looked them over.

"Perhaps because I enjoy landscapes most. I have always thought heart shows through an artist's work."

"I wish I still had the landscapes," Mr Scott said regretfully.

"Mr Scott was kind enough to sell some of them for me."

"My offer still stands if you ever decide to paint again."

She shook her head. "You are most kind. But I have no time. I cannot leave my mother for so long." She looked out the window. "And it looks as if the storm has let up. It was lovely to see you again, Mr Scott. Thank you for the shelter."

They walked quietly up the rain soaked hill to her rooms.

Mr Abbott spoke: "What other landscapes have you painted?"

"Most were down by the Avon near the Pulteney Bridge—I especially love the spring and summer blooms around, and the challenge of capturing running water was always a favourite."

"Any others?"

She barked a slight deprecating laugh. "I confess to trying to imitate the Renaissance Masters' techniques, except with architecture not people. The park in front of the Royal Crescent was my favourite medium for that disastrous attempt."

"Do you have any of those?"

"I believe a few may be stuffed into a trunk in the attic. Which is where they belong, I assure you!"

"Would you be willing to paint one for me before I go? Commissioned, of course."

"No," she bent her head quietly as they reached the door.

"I'm not asking out of pity."

She looked up at him then. How had he read her thoughts?

"I don't know if I could finish before you leave."

"I will pick you up early tomorrow to give us the best chance."

Before she could protest he tipped his hat with a huge grin on his face and ran off.

Chapter Four

"Do you think it will do any good?" Millicent asked her cousin
Henrietta.

"All we can do is put them in each other's way and let nature take its
course."

"I suppose so. If only Mr Abbott were not obliged to leave for
A...A..." she trailed off, searching for the word.

"America. From the look of the two of them together, I would think he
would offer for her before he leaves. It had better be all he does.
Smelling of April and May, those two."

"I am afraid she will feel obligated to me. The girl is more headstrong
than she appears."

"She need not leave you. He will not be gone very long. Sir Charles
assured me of that or I would have insisted he remain," the Dowager said
reassuringly.

"That assumes they take to each other. I only wish she would not be
left in such dire straits when I am gone."

"Now, Millicent, I assured you I would look after her."

"I know, Cousin. But she will outlive the both of us, Lord willing, and
who will look after her then? I began to suggest she attempt to contact
her cousin Kendall, but she was vehemently opposed to it."

"After the way the family behaved towards you, I cannot be surprised. I
would feel much the same."

"Perhaps I should attempt to write to him myself, though I am not
certain I can manage with my shakes. Their grandfather had intended the
two of them to be matched at one point. How things change," she

reflected sadly.

"I do not think we are at the point to be grovelling. Let us see if my grandson comes up to scratch before we do anything unbecoming. I have a fair notion that Andrew was besotted at first sight."

"Gwen has nothing to offer him," she said, frowning.

"It depends on what one is looking for. I assure you, Andrew has had every eligible cap thrown at him. If it was power or wealth he desired, he could have had it any time this age."

"If only I was assured of her, I would be easy. She does not believe herself to be a worthy match. He seems a very fine gentleman."

"Let us hope my grandson will convince her. He is not without charms, I assure you."

"If I were younger I would have swooned at the sight of him," Millicent agreed.

"Oh nothing so vulgar, I hope dear," she said with a hint of distaste.

The door opened and Gwen came in damp with her hair unkempt.

"Did that rapscallion grandson of mine abandon you on the doorstep?" she asked, looking for him.

"Yes, I mean no, ma'am. I would not say abandoned, but he did leave."

"Well! I never! He was raised better than that," she exclaimed.

"Oh, don't be cross with him. I believe he had another errand. He was very attentive to me all afternoon."

The Dowager eyed her dishevelled state. "Not too attentive, I hope."

Gwen blushed and self-consciously smoothed down her unruly hair. "We were caught in the storm. Shall I make tea?" She began walking towards the kitchen in hope of escaping the Dowager's inquisition.

"Hettie is already seeing to it. Come sit and tell me about your walk."

She forced herself to smile and sat obediently. Hettie brought in the tea tray, and Gwen poured for everyone.

"So what do you think of my handsome grandson?"

Gwen swallowed her sip of tea too quickly and had to hold back a hiccough.

The Dowager looked her over thoughtfully, waiting for her answer. Her mother pulled her head up from where it was resting to look.

"I think he is a very entertaining companion." Gwen carefully selected a biscuit and did not look up, though she could feel their eyes upon her.

"That is all?"

No, but she wasn't about to say he was the most handsome, witty, above-her-touch man she had ever met.

"He likes my paintings."

"Gwen, you are being purposefully..." Her mother wrinkled her brow and put her head down again.

"Obtuse, Mama? I am not sure what your expectations were of an afternoon walk, but we enjoyed a nice exercise, a beautiful view and pleasant conversation."

The Dowager humphed. "Sounds perfectly mundane."

"Do you have plans for tomorrow?"

"I believe he wishes me to paint something for him."

"Oh, Gwen! You haven't...." She searched for the right word but couldn't find it. "...Done that in years. What shall you...?" Her face grew frustrated.

"Paint? Whatever Mr Abbott wishes. He is commissioning it."

"My grandson commissioned a painting?" the Dowager said with surprise.

"He did, ma'am."

"Oh, dear. This is serious indeed." She flashed a smile at her cousin. "I will see you in the morning it seems. I best be away, dear."

~*~

Andrew hurried back to the colourist's shop and availed himself of every possible canvas, brush and pigment Mr Scott thought Miss Lambert might desire. After arranging for the supplies to be delivered, he then went to the Pulteney Bridge to examine the various options for her masterpiece. Unsatisfied, he walked back towards his house on the Circus and diverted himself along Brock Street towards the park in front of the Royal Crescent.

"This will do nicely," he said to himself as he envisioned a lovely day with Miss Lambert. "A picnic, a blanket, her canvas right there. A lovely day it will be." He looked up to the sky, begging for cooperative weather. "Except perhaps enough of a breeze to blow Miss Lambert's wild hair about."

No. He did not need the temptation. It was all he could do this afternoon to keep his hands out of it when it was tumbling about her. He sighed. She did not think of him as more than a friend. He was only supposed to be providing a brief divertissement anyway. He was leaving for America in two days and only God knew how long he would be gone. He looked to the sky again. "As an arbiter of humour, I must say I have to appreciate how diverted you must be."

He turned and walked back towards number twenty-one, nevertheless excited for tomorrow. It was nice to feel a sense of purpose again, even if it would be of short duration. He headed straight for Cook to order up a basket of delicacies worthy of a queen. He was in trouble, he must acknowledge. All of his thoughts were on Miss Lambert, and how he could bring a smile to her face. He would be miserable when he had to leave her, but if she enjoyed herself, nay forgot herself, for a few days his misery would be worth it.

She did not flirt with him whatsoever, and while not piqued, he certainly felt challenged. Usually he at least ranked some courtesy flirting from ladies. What was it about him that kept her from desiring him? He was not an eyesore; at least he did not think he was repulsive. Was he too familiar? He had never succumbed to the old adage of playing hard to get. He enjoyed conversing and laughing…perhaps that was his downfall. He treated the ladies as he would a friend. Did he need to be more romantic or obvious? He was afraid he would look a fool, but he likely would not be able to stop himself.

~*~

Gwen had barely finished her chores when she heard a knock at the door. Could Mr Abbott have arrived so early? He said morning, but to town folk that generally meant after noon. Her mother had barely dressed and come downstairs. Gwen needed to change, as she still had on her ragged gown on that she wore for housework. She opened the door to find the Dowager before her.

"Good morning, Your Grace."

"Good morning, dear." The Dowager made her way inside. "You best change quickly. I am to send you to meet Andrew in the carriage."

"The carriage?" No one used carriages in Bath. The terrain was steep and the town small. If a person were unable or disinclined to walk they called for a chair. She had almost understood the carriage for the ball, but in a day dress?

"Those were his instructions. Hurry along."

Why the mystery? She wondered but did as she was told. Her day gown was little better than her other, but it was the newest she had. She kissed her mother goodbye and climbed into the waiting carriage.

The drive was very short—only to the Royal Crescent—and Gwendolyn shook her head. She was not accustomed to such luxuries. The footman opened the door and pointed to where Mr Abbott was setting up an array of painting supplies.

"Good morning, Miss Lambert. I hope this will do." He beamed, pleased with himself.

"Good morning Mr Abbott. Gracious! It looks as if you purchased the entire store," she exclaimed as she surveyed the variety of canvas, pigments and brushes. He already had a beautiful new easel set up for her. She must have died and was caught in purgatory watching someone that looked like her living her dream.

"Well," Mr Abbott interrupted her thoughts. "Say something please. Is this acceptable? I could not find a satisfactory place by the Bridge, so I selected your other favourite."

"Acceptable? It is beyond anything I could have imagined. If you wish for me to paint the Royal Crescent, however, we'd best get started."

"We? No, no. I am merely here to see to your comfort. You paint, I entertain. You'd best begin." He motioned her on. "As it is, it sounds like you might not have time for breaks. But inform me when you need sustenance and I will bring it to you."

"Am I not allowed to rest, then?" she asked wide-eyed, still unsure of when he was teasing.

"Of course," he said with crinkled eyes and a devillish smile. "When you finish."

She gave him a perplexed look and turned to her task. She carefully selected a canvas, trying not to think about the fact that he was going to be watching her all day. His focused gaze was disconcerting. Fortunately, as soon as the frame was in place, all of her thoughts were on her art. She prepped the canvas then sketched a rough drawing of the building, and concentrated on the proper mixture of colours. How could she have forgotten the recipes for Bath stone and the sky and the grass? She had known them by heart. She desperately wanted to make this beautiful for him. Her hands began to shake and she fought back tears.

"Miss Lambert? Did I forget a colour? I can retrieve it at once! I relied solely on Mr Scott to choose. I never knew there were so many hues of yellow." He was instantly before her, exaggerating his concern. "Tell me what your heart desires and you shall have it immediately! I am at your disposal."

She giggled despite herself. He had a way of making everything seem humourous.

"No, forgive me. You thought of everything, but I do not know if I can do this anymore."

"Of course you can. Splash some paint up there and see what happens. It will be like riding a horse. It will come right back to you."

She laughed, "One does not splash paint, Mr Abbott."

"Then show me what you do with it. Teach me. I have always admired art, but never had the patience for lessons."

She sighed. "Very well. But it is the colours I am worried about."

"I never cared for Bath stone personally, so I will be happy with whatever you choose."

"You shall find yourself with a picture not fit for a nursery wall, sir."

"Yes, well, one must have to have a nursery to worry about that." He coughed into his hand and feigned great interest in her picture.

She selected Indian yellow, ceruse white and black lead and began mixing the colours with the oil and turpentine. She started over several times, but finally settled on a mixture. She then mixed ultramarine blue with chalk and began the sky. When the brush hit the canvas, she found her rhythm. He was right.

~*~

Was he out of his mind? Andrew sat back on the blanket and watched Miss Lambert work. She was the most exquisite being he had ever seen and she was completely engrossed in her art, ignoring him. That was not how he had envisioned the day, but she was happy. He watched her transform as she took the brush in her hand; she was radiant, confident, and smiling. And that made him happy. When he could no longer take it, he paced around her for a while and, eventually, he sorted through the basket of food and found some fruit he could distract her with.

He waved a strawberry in front of her mouth and had to shove it in to get her attention.

"Oh! Thank you," she said with the berry lodged in her teeth.

"I thought you might be hungry," he said sheepishly and shoved his hands in his pockets.

"I am, actually. I have not yet breakfasted."

"Take a break and eat."

"Why thank you, Master," she said coolly.

She eyed the canvas, which was now a muddle of blues, yellows and greens.

"I suppose a few minutes won't hurt. It will allow the initial layer to dry a bit."

He helped her take a seat on the blanket and began to fill a plate for her.

"How much is there left to do?"

"Several hours' worth."

Hours? So much for this brilliant idea. He wanted her to pay attention

51

to him. He was desperate.

"I see." He must have frowned.

"Oil paintings are not normally painted in a day, Mr Abbott. I am doing my best to use thin layers, but most oil paintings do not fully cure for years, decades even."

"Decades?" he asked in astonishment.

"I only need to outline the buildings, and the rest I will finish at home after this layer dries."

Thank God.

"You must be bored to tears. You needn't wait here with me."

"Not at all. I am fascinated. But will it be ready in time for my departure?"

"I will do my best."

"Why is this one of your favourite places to paint?"

She looked towards the magnificent structure, "I suppose the challenging façade with its iconic columns, defying the bounds of symmetry, standing tall in grandeur over the valley. I normally prefer natural landscapes, but I confess a weakness for Palladian structure."

"Then Bath should be your heaven on Earth. I will have to remember that when rebuilding the plantation house, so if you ever visit you will wish to paint it."

"If I ever have cause to visit, I will happily paint it."

"I can give you cause."

Her eyes met his in question for a moment and flickered with some unrecognized emotion, but then she averted her eyes. Her pulse beat strong in her neck and a flush crept over her visible skin, yet she remained silent and looking away. Did she not welcome his attentions? Had he been too bold? He was not one to waste time feeling self-conscious, but her response mattered to him very much.

After a slightly awkward pause, she spoke. "I envy you, Mr Abbott."

"That is something I've not heard before."

"I suppose not in the way you imagine, but to be able to pick and go anywhere you choose at any moment." She began to stand and he rose to help her.

"It has its benefits. For instance, when my sisters or grandmother suddenly have brilliant plans for me."

She picked up her brush and dipped it in the paint. "Such as escorting a poor relation about town," she said with a smile.

"I refuse to countenance that remark. Besides, I would not have agreed to something which I did not wish to participate." He watched carefully as her brush stilled. It went back to work after a few moments, but she did not respond. Again, she chose to ignore his hinting, and boldly at that.

He was near, too near, standing directly behind her as she worked, taking in her scent of…he sniffed. What was that fragrance? Lemons, lavender and turpentine? He leaned forward and inhaled deeply. He had the strongest urge to pull her in his arms kiss her.

She spun about and almost covered him with her palette of paint. She drew it back and fell forward into him. He had to force himself to right her, when all he longed to do was give the old harpies an eyeful. Nothing went on in this town that the 'Bath quizzes' did not know about, and that would not be fair to leave Miss Lambert's reputation ruined when he was leaving two days hence.

"Pardon me, I was trying to see your view as you paint."

"Oh, by all means then." The innocent miss scooted over to make room for him. He moved closer, against his better judgement, and was completely enthralled by her creation. The picture was beginning to take form, no longer splotches of colour, but a glorious imitation of the scene before him. It was wonderful. And so was the painting.

"Is it so dreadful you have no words?" she said with self-deprecating humour.

"On the contrary, I am in awe that you were able to make me think Bath stone glorious."

She laughed. It was the most melodious sound he had ever heard. Her face lit up and she forgot to be cautious. He wanted a portrait of that to take with him on his travels.

"I confess I was shocked when you selected this spot for the painting."

He shrugged a shoulder. "I wanted to see you paint, and this seemed the best location."

She shied again. "I apologise, I had not thought of your comfort. I tend to forget myself when I hold one of these in my hand." She waved the brush dramatically.

"There was no discomfort, I assure you." Save his pride.

"I would love to hear about your travels one day, Mr Abbott. I may live vicariously through you."

"That would bore you, indeed."

"No, please. I long to hear of other places. All of my visions of places are from books. To hear an account first hand would be delightful."

"I could not do justice to them, for I am no poet." He suddenly had an idea for a gift.

"There." She placed one last stroke on the canvas with a flourish. "I believe I may be finished for now."

"You are certain you are not stopping so soon for my benefit?"

"No," she smiled. "I am certain."

"Shall I have everything delivered to your home?"

"Thank you, yes. I shall place the finishing touches tonight after this dries."

"I will have it seen to." He waved the footmen over and directed the transport of the supplies back to Miss Lambert's home.

"Shall we walk?" She eyed her work on the easel then looked towards the footmen with distrust. "It will be fine. They will guard it with their lives."

She nodded, unconvinced, and hesitantly took his proffered arm. She reached up to adjust her bonnet and left behind a smudge of paint. Heaven help him, he was jealous of that streak of jade that matched her eyes. He took out his handkerchief and wiped it off. Her dimples formed on her cheeks and he fought the impulse to reach down and kiss them both. He was utterly lost. He took a deep breath and forced his concentration away from kissing her. He straightened and walked briskly, likely dragging her, but he needed some time to cool down and clear his head. One more day, then his head would be clearer than he wanted.

Chapter Five

How could she have forgotten herself for so long? A day that had been magical was how. She shook her head as she placed her bonnet on the table and ran in to check on her mother. The Dowager and Mr Abbott quickly excused themselves and left, and Gwen set about tending to her mother who looked poorly.

"Are you unwell, Mama?"

"I confess I'm very tired. Cousin Henrietta was not taxing in the least, but I am simply not used to being up so long."

"Forgive me, Mama. I forgot myself and all sense of time."

"I gather you enjoyed yourself?" her mother said with a kind smile.

"I did, Mama. Mr Abbott is everything kind and a delightful companion. I have much work to do on the painting tonight to have it ready for tomorrow, however."

"Well, I will not hold you up. I would like to retire if you do not mind."

Gwen's face wrinkled with concern, but she nodded and helped her mother to her room.

When she came back downstairs, the footmen were placing all of the canvases, the easel and paints about the parlour. It overwhelmed the small room.

"Oh, my goodness," she exclaimed. "I did not know Mr Abbott intended to bring everything here. I insist you take the extra supplies with you."

"Oh, no, miss. He was very adamant that we leave everything here."

She blew out a frustrated breath that sent her errant wisps of hair flying.

"Very well. I will take it up with him myself in the morning."

The footmen left after gingerly placing the painting on the easel. She sat and had a cup of tea while staring at it. Not too shabby for six years without practice. She laughed to herself. She was not sure that Mr Abbott was a connoisseur of art at all. She could literally splash paint on the canvas and he would declare it exquisite. It would serve him right if she did.

What had he meant by flirting with her so openly? She had thought he was flirting at least. She could not flirt back—she would make a fool of herself and it would change everything about this magical moment. And her heart would long for something it could not have.

Gwen was surprised he did not realise he was toying with her. He did not seem a libertine. It was likely just Society's way. Even if he were honourable, they both knew nothing could come of such an unequal match. She sighed wistfully. It did no good to long for something that could never be. She had enjoyed his company very much. She has not had such fun in years—if ever—and she was grateful for that at least. She would cherish this time and his friendship and have a precious memory to hold onto.

She stood and placed an apron over her gown, and began the finishing touches to her masterpiece, trying not to think about the moment she thought Mr Abbott was going to kiss her. When he hadn't, she'd had to turn away to gather her wits and not pull his head down to hers.

It was dawn before she was satisfied. She prayed that the day would be dry so the paint would have a chance at setting. Not likely in Bath! She took her weary body up the stairs to wash and change. She still had chores to complete before Mr Abbott arrived for his picture.

Knock, knock. Gwen jumped from the chair she had unknowingly fallen asleep in. After a moment's disorientation, she rubbed her aching neck and realised that the Dowager and Mr Abbott must have arrived. She pointlessly attempted to right her hair, and answered the door.

"Good morning, Your Grace, Mr Abbott." She curtsied and opened the door wide for them to enter.

"Good morning, Miss Lambert. Is it finished? May I see it?" Mr Abbott asked excitedly.

"It is," she said, unable to suppress a grin. "Follow me." She led them into the parlour where the finished work of art stood brilliantly on the easel.

"I am astonished! This is the same picture from yesterday? I can scarcely believe it!"

"The very same that you declared glorious only yesterday."

His eyes danced at her.

"I'll have you know I was tempted to splash paint all over it and call it finished."

He barked an appreciative laugh and looked at her meaningfully. Her heart began to thud in her chest. She was both unnerved and enamoured by the feeling it gave her.

Would that she could have captured that look on his face. Perhaps she would attempt to do so when he left. Portraits had never been her forté, but she had never been so inspired by a face before.

He broke their gaze and looked back towards the painting. His look of appreciation was higher praise than any words he could have uttered.

"I definitely prefer your version to the real thing. It is perfect."

She had added personal touches to the scene—hints of colours around the park, blooms on the tree and brilliant hues that captured the sun's effect on the clouds.

"That is high praise, indeed, Mr Abbott."

"Miss Lambert, would you mind taking a short walk with me?
She looked behind her to where her mother and the Dowager were happily chatting. She nodded. He held the door for her and then offered his arm. She noticed he picked up a parcel from the table and put it under his other arm.

They walked in silence for some streets. Both were content arm in arm, but sad over Andrew's impending departure.

"Forgive the indelicate question, but how much does one pay for a painting? There is no need to sell me a bargain."

"It is my birthday gift to you."

"That was not our agreement!" he protested.

"I insist. I assure you, being able to paint again was payment enough."

"Very well, I thank you."

They walked on in silence. Eventually, Mr Abbott spoke. "I do not suppose there is any chance you would come with me?"

Gwen felt all of the air rush from her lungs, and her eyes filled with moisture before she could think to stop it.

He turned and took both shoulders in his hands and lowered his face to hers searching with worry. "Never mind, I take it back! I did not mean to offend you! Please say something, Miss Lambert."

She rapped him on the arm playing off her hurt. She would not argue with him on his departure. It did not occur to him that his offer was highly improper. She'd had enough of those kind of offers, and she could not blame him for not wanting to marry her.

"I'm fine," She did her best to smile and not look hurt.

"You don't seem fine." He eyed her suspiciously but straightened and held his arm out. He stopped when he realized he had dropped the parcel he'd been carrying.

She looked at it curiously but refrained from saying anything whilst trying to compose herself.

"You know I cannot leave my mother," she said quietly.

"I assumed as much." He shoved the parcel into her hands. "This is for you."

"What is this?"

"A small gift to keep you company in my absence." He smiled rakishly.

"Go on open it!"

She removed the ribbon and paper to reveal two beautiful leather-bound books.

"Mr Abbott! I could never accept such a gift," she said, as she lovingly fingered the covers of *Robinson Crusoe* and *Gulliver's Travels*.

"I thought you could read them and imagine me off on a wild adventure of my own."

"Is that not the story where the man is shipwrecked and lives on a deserted island for decades?"

"Perhaps not the best choice."

"Speaking of gifts, I insist you take the extra painting supplies as well. Your footmen mistakenly thought you meant to leave them."

She finally dared to look him in the eye. That was a mistake. His face showed genuine hurt.

"I apologise. I had not considered the impropriety. It is not as if I gave you jewels."

She blushed.

"I was merely excited for you to read two of my favourite books."

"It was very kind of you, Mr Abbott, but it would not be proper." She attempted to shove them back towards him. He pushed them back.

"Then we shall say you are borrowing them. I will not hear otherwise."

She laughed and shook her head. "You are impossible."

"Indeed. You are just now coming to that realisation?"

They turned and walked a while longer.

"How long shall you be gone?"

"I have no idea. My father seems to believe the property is in need of a good deal of work."

"I see."

"Will you write to me while I am gone?"

"I, I..." What could she say?

"Am I being improper? You have no guardian to ask permission, and you yourself pointed out you were no longer in need of chaperonage."

"It isn't that." She toyed with her stray hair. "I don't know how to post a letter to America, or if I could afford to do so. How long would a letter even take?"

"It will take weeks or months, I am certain. No matter, I will see to everything. When you have a letter written send it to my father's house and it will be posted for you."

"I don't know..." she hesitated.

"Please. Do not make me beg. It will make my time there less lonely and I will have something to look forward to."

She looked at him with confusion. Why would he want her letters? Why was he interested in anything she had to say to the point of fronting the postage?

"Very well. I doubt there will be anything of interest to report from the fast town of Bath, but if you insist, I shall write so often you will regret you ever asked."

She was rewarded with a smile that made her knees feel weak.

"I am much obliged." He bowed and took her hands and bestowed a kiss on them, but he didn't let go. Her pulse raced with anticipation. "I shall look forward to each and every one. If you need anything at all while I am gone, promise me you will ask my grandmother or father."

"That will not be necessary."

"Promise me. I will not let go until you do."

She sighed.

"Remember, I am impossible."

"Indeed. Very well, Mr Abbott. I would like to thank you for your friendship. I shall cherish your kindness to me long past your time in Bath."

Friendship. Why was that such an inapt word for her feelings? He lingered, still holding her hand and brushing his thumb over it lightly. She was about to come undone, but could not force herself to let go. When it was time to part, he kissed her hand again meaningfully with a look she would never forget.

"Goodbye, Mr Abbott."

"Until later, Miss Lambert."

~*~

"Are you terribly sad, dear?"

She turned back from where she was gazing out the window at the empty street. It was nearly time for the Dowager's afternoon visit—the time when Mr Abbott had called daily for the past week.

"A little, I suppose. It's funny how accustomed I became to his company in one short week."

"I felt certain he would have d...d...d..." Her mother again searched for the right word and became frustrated and embarrassed when she could not remember.

Gwen hurried to cover the mistake as she had done often of late.

"Declared himself? No, Mama. He did speak some nonsense about me visiting America, but he spoke only of friendship. He did ask me to correspond with him. I hope you will not think me fast."

She looked at her mother to smile reassuringly, but Mama's eyes were filled with tears. Gwen went to her and held her. She had become the protective, comforting one, a reversal of roles. Her mother's eyes held fear. She was losing control of her body and could do nothing about it.

"Do not worry for my feelings, Mama. I had no expectations of such a grand match."

"I'm afraid, Gwen."

"I know, Mama. I know." She had to hold back the sob that was suffocating her throat. "But do not be afraid for me at least."

She held her in a tight embrace, rubbing her mother's hair and back. Her mother laid her head on Gwen's shoulder, which seemed to calm her until the knock on the door came.

When the Dowager arrived, she looked more sombre than usual. She must be feeling Mr Abbott's departure keenly as well, Gwen thought.

"Is everything all right, Your Grace?"

"Nothing serious." She waved her hand dismissively. "I have an unbecoming case of the sullens."

Gwen refrained from comment, but nodded understanding. She felt glum herself.

"Where shall you go today, Gwen?"

"I'm not certain. I think I would like to paint a little. Something small." She was able to keep an impassive face. Hopefully they would not ask to see her work. She would never confess to painting Mr Abbott.

"Run along then. We will chat when you return." The Dowager took a seat. "Oh, Gwen," she called after her as she fished around in her reticule. "This is for you." She handed Gwen a letter.

Gwen dipped a curtsy and hurried off to her room to read it. She felt the need to escape more acutely today. With her mother growing worse and no one to help her, she needed the brief reprieve. She did not know how she could handle the situation if she did not have the Dowager.

She took a seat and opened the letter.

Dearest Miss Lambert,

Do you miss me yet? I wrote this letter before I left, for I hope you will miss me dreadfully and long to have something to remember my unparalleled wit by. I am sure I am at this moment toiling away in the humid heat of Washington, dreadfully sunburnt and wrinkled. I will have by now rebuilt one wing of the house single-handedly, having felled each tree and hand-crafted each board with master craftsmanship. I will also perform the task of smithy and forge the nails with my bare hands. I would that I had your skill with paint and brush that I could capture my own work of art, for I am certain you imagine I exaggerate.

Your obedient servant,

Andrew Abbott

"I'm surprised he doesn't claim that as well. Silly man," she said out loud, laughing. She penned a reply to send with the Dowager today.

Dear Mr Abbott,

For shame. I never knew what I was missing before you upturned my world. Now I expect you to arrive my doorstep any moment with a grandiose plan for the day. Instead, I am ill-content to do my chores, if you can imagine. Caring for my mother is the only unburdensome part of my day, I cannot bring myself to jest of her. I fear she is weakening in mind and body and there is nothing to be done. I hope your hands have not become rough and calloused, but I confess I admire such a skilled man. In fact, there are many needs around here I will happily compile a list for your edification that you may complete upon your return. Do make haste.

Affectionately,

Miss Gwendolyn Lambert

She folded the note and readied it to send with the Dowager. Then she hurried with anticipation of painting a small portrait of Mr Abbott. He had left six canvases of varying sizes, and she would use them sparingly to make them last. However, she could not help wanting to capture his likeness. She would likely not see him for a very long time—if ever again—and wanted something to remember him by when she was old and grey. She scoffed at herself: already an old maid!

She walked to one of her old favourite spots. One of the few places she had not been with Mr Abbott. She trekked all the way down to the Avon and found a shady tree in the park where she set up her painting things. She had always adored water. Watching it run and sparkle had always been soothing to her. Another of Earth's majesties that many took for granted.

She quickly began to apply the paint lovingly over the charcoal sketch she had made of Mr Abbott as soon as he had left. The likeness was remarkable, and made her heart clinch with aching as it longed for him. She must try to find a way to cease her thoughts and fantasies, for she knew nothing could come of them. She would hold onto that week with him fondly for the remainder of her days. Even if his offer was not a proper one, he had given her a momentary escape from the tedium of chores and invalidism. If only her heart had remained unaffected, the week would have been perfect.

She studied the blue eyes that held their signature twinkle, surrounded by long lashes and a few small scars he must have received in the wars. His nose was not perfect, but had a minor bend to it, and his mouth held a slight upturn to one side indicating his ready humour.

How she needed that humour right now. "Oh, Andrew," she whispered his name intimately as she thought of him to herself, "I shall never look at life the same way again." How she longed for his comforting presence, his strength. Somehow, everything had felt right when he was near, that it would all turn out right. She brushed back an errant tear and tried to not allow the desolation she felt overcome her.

She wished she had painted the picture larger, for the miniature hardly did him justice. She shook her head. A larger picture would only make everything worse. She chided herself. She had no right to have painted him without his permission, but she was not ready to confess such to him. Perhaps when he returned she would give it to him as a gift. Or perhaps not.

~*~

She hurriedly packed up her things and headed back to her home. The tea-tray had already been set out and her mother looked up at her with sadness in her eyes.

"What's the matter, Mama?"

"I will let Cousin Henrietta tell you herself."

Gwendolyn looked at the Dowager with concern.

"I am sorry to tell you that I will be leaving for a while."

"Oh, no! Is something amiss?"

"My youngest granddaughter, Andrew's sister, Elinor, is having a difficult confinement. Their sister, Sarah, is also having some difficulties. Sir Charles and I are leaving in the morning to offer our assistance."

"I am sorry to hear it. Will they be all right?"

"I think so." She took a sip of her tea. "Gwendolyn, I want you to keep me abreast of all the happenings here in Bath." She looked at Gwen meaningfully. "There will still be someone at the house who will post your letters for you to me, or elsewhere." She winked at her. "I must be off now to finish packing." She walked over and gave Gwen's mother a kiss on the cheek and a reassuring squeeze of the hand. "I shall return soon, Cousin."

Her mother nodded, but tears were streaming down her face. She was shaking and had that look of terror in her eyes again. Gwen was not feeling confident about the Dowager leaving herself. Genuine fear washed over her. She was now left to deal with things on her own. Would she be able to manage?

"Gwen?"

"Yes, Mama?"

"I need to write a letter. Would you please bring me a quill and…"

"Yes, I will bring the things to you." She set up the quill, ink and paper. "Shall I write it for you?"

"No, I would like to do this myself."

Her mother had not written in years, but she would not argue if she wished to try.

"Very well."

Chapter Six

Andrew was miserable. He suffered seasickness, and he suffered sickness of the heart. He had not wanted to leave Miss Lambert. He'd had that gnawing feeling inside that something was wrong. He had never felt this level of attraction to anyone before—and he had been around long enough to know his own feelings. But he could not read hers. She never seemed to think he was being serious. But he had been in earnest, and she had ignored his amorous overtures. He'd not planned to blurt out for her to join him. He knew it was impossible with her mother's condition.

The triplets had been beautiful and amusing, but they had never been more than a passing fancy for him. It might have turned into something more had the stars aligned in the right way, but they had not. He would describe it more akin to a shooting star—a flash of brilliance that burnt out in the blink of an eye. With Miss Lambert, he felt strongly enough that he would fight for her and make her see that she belonged with him when the time was right, whenever that might be.

Now he had weeks with nowhere to go but to his lonely cabin, with his lonely thoughts of a stunning redhead. He wished he could have remained to alleviate some of her burdens, but he had already given his word. Hopefully her mother would survive until he returned, for the thought of her on her own...he shuddered. No, the world was not kind to beautiful, destitute, females. And one whose family had fallen from grace at that. She had few choices open to her. He felt an unhealthy measure of protectiveness, but she had no one. He had asked his father and his grandmother to look after her, and he trusted that they would.

And he would have to make sure that his time away from her was short. How hard could it be to find a steward and a carpenter? He would literally rebuild the house himself if that was what was necessary in order to return to Miss Lambert. It might be only be a one-roomed house....

He still had work to do to convince her he was in earnest. He pulled out his pen and paper. He would write to her as often as possible, or as long as his ink and paper supply lasted. He would not allow her to forget him or to second-guess his feelings for her. Perhaps they would pass some returning ships and he could send his letters sooner. He wished he could have seen her smile when she'd read his first letter. He could just hear her laughing, attributing a name to him such as ridiculous or impossible, and her kissable dimples would wink at him.

Miss Lambert,

I am happy to report that I have survived an entire day aboard ship. That leaves an unthinkable number of days until I arrive. I sought passage on the fastest ship I could find, but the captain tells me it will take at least three weeks regardless, even if the winds are favourable. Heaven help me, for the sea makes me green. I know it dampens your ardour to hear thus of me. But please pray for calm seas, though enough wind to push the sails at record pace...

I have become very well acquainted with the side rails and deck. They do not speak much except to mock me. Until I may write again.

Your obedient servant,
Andrew Abbott

He arrived after four weeks at sea. He thanked the captain, the heavens, and kissed the dirty American landing when he set foot on it. He'd heard horror stories of folk taking several months to reach the Americas, and was grateful for his miserably short trip. He immediately hired a horse and set off southward for River's Bend, instead of finding a small boat to row onto the property. If he never saw a boat again it would be too soon. He thought he remembered the direction. If nothing else, he would follow the river.

It was a warm day, and the smells in the air were sweet from the fragrant foliage of honeysuckle and jasmine which wafted to his nose from the breeze. It felt magnificent to be on horseback again. He dreaded the return, but he would not dwell on that until it was time. By then, he would gladly suffer the sea to be with Miss Lambert again.

It was a short ride, one that his father and sister had made almost daily. He pulled through the gates after the refreshing gallop, but he wasn't prepared for the sight before him. The entire façade of the house was demolished. Some rebuilding had taken place, and some of the structure held a framework for future repairs to come, but most of the house looked uninhabitable. He felt sick and disgusted. This had been done out of an act of retaliation because of the anger towards the British after they burnt Washington. There were so many barbaric acts that came after battles—few of them resulted from rational thought. He had seen them time and again, whether from soldiers scuffling in the barracks, seeking out women and drink, or worse as had happened after the battle at Cuidad Rodrigo.

He dismounted and tied his horse to the tree. The workers must all be in the fields, for there was no sign of life in the ruin of the house. He was thankful Elly was not here to see this. She had suffered enough. He could not believe the damage done, and it had been three years. Three years, and it appeared little to no work had been done.

He stepped gingerly into the entryway, where beams stood to hold up the rear wing of the house which had not fallen. The front half of the house was only a frame. It looked as though some care had been taken to clean away the ashes and soot, and a portion of the house appeared to be partially intact, at least. He stopped, and thought better of exploring on his own without finding Abe. He had no idea what parts of the mansion were safe to wander through.

His hopes sank. This was going to require more work than he had imagined. He wondered if there would be a place for him to live, or if he would have to pitch a tent like he had when in the Army. He set out to look for Abe, when all he wanted to do was have a bath and a drink.

Miss Lambert,

I have finally arrived. Summer here is hotter than I ever imagined it could be and survive it. It is similar to the heat in the Mediterranean, but more humid.

Thankfully, the workers here do not mind if you roll up your shirt sleeves and loosen your cravat. Abe has continued to manage the fields beautifully, but the house is in need of much repair. How I wish I had brought a female to see to the decorations, for carpets, window hangings and upholstery, for colour coordination is not in my repertoire. However, my father put me in charge so he will have to be content with my choices....

Social life is different here, though not so different. There are many

British and Americans with marriageable daughters, eager to welcome me to their table for their sakes. Should I tell them I have no title and do not own River's Bend? Most Americans are transplanted from England or the Continent. People are in general very open-mannered and friendly—an interesting but amusing change from English society.

I have already begun interviewing stewards to oversee the running of the estate, and have hired carpenters to finish rebuilding the manor house which was devastated by the fires. I am spending my spare time hunting or fishing, riding the fields, or looking at blueprints, anxious to have this settled so I may return. I have placed your painting over the mantle in the wing of the house that is habitable. I envision your portrait of River's Bend hanging there one day. For now, I content myself with glorious Bath stone.

The view this evening is serene, as I sit on the porch drinking a glass of cold lemonade, recalling the last time I drank it in your delightful company. I do wish you were here to enjoy the picturesque view. I will attempt to paint it with words, but will hardly do it justice.

The remains of the house overlook a bend in a wide river, the colour of which is muddy brown at times and green at others. There are tall pine trees, intermingled with elms, oaks, birches and weeping willows. Magnolia trees are scattered through the gardens, their white blooms scenting the thick air. Crickets and cicada sing their songs to me as I swat the mosquitoes providing accompaniment for their tunes. Kindly pray for more breezes.

Our property is nearby a lovely estate called Mt. Vernon, where the first American President, George Washington, lived. He established a fine gristmill and distillery (which also burned in 1814), and his grandson-in-law Lewis has kindly shared advice and recommendations for stewards and builders. It is in their best interests to do so since we will be away much of the time. Now my objective is to obtain a secret whisky recipe from him.

Wishing you were here,

Andrew Abbott

~*~

"Gwen! Gwen! Where is Edmund?" She heard a panicked voice from her bedroom. She threw back the covers and ran to her mother's room.

"Mama?"

"Edmund! Edmund! I want to go home!" Her mother looked directly at her but didn't see her.

"Who is Edmund, Mama?" Was she speaking of her brother who had died as a child?

Again, her mother looked at her, but didn't seem to recognise her.

"Edmund!" She called out to him again and was growing angry, and rattled the door to escape.

"Take me to him. I need to go to Castlebury!"

"Castlebury? You have not been there since you were a girl, Mama." She had to be dreaming.

"Take me there. Now! He needs me!"

Her mother's face turned fierce, and she grabbed Gwen's hands and shook them with uncharacteristic strength. What was she to do? Mama was clearly out of her senses. She needed a diversion, and quickly. Rationalizing was getting Gwen nowhere; she tried agreeing with her instead.

"Yes, of course, Mama, we can go and look for Edmund, but you cannot wear your night clothes. Shall we return upstairs and dress you?"

Her mother nodded blankly, apparently happy that Gwen was finally listening to her. Gwen hoped the older woman would grow tired or wake up. Fortunately by the time they had returned upstairs and she'd sat her mother on the bed, her mama did not resist being tucked in.

Gwen returned to her own room, sat on the edge of her bed, and began to cry. Her mother was worsening and she had no idea of how to help her. She would send for Mr Norman tomorrow, but was unhopeful of any help.

She found herself unable to return to sleep, and longed to rise and paint to help her clear her head, but could ill afford the expense of lighting a taper for the rest of the night. Instead, she wrote a letter. Somehow writing the words helped her imagine she was not as alone in the world as she felt.

Mr Abbott,

Mother is worsening. She has begun falling and wavers much in her gait. Her memory is unsteady. Some days she looks at me as if she doesn't know who I am. Other days she asks after my father, or for my brother who died in the war. She is mostly normal during the day, but night times reveal a completely different character, one who seems to reside somewhere thirty to forty years past.

I have little hope for her improvement. I fear by the time my letter reaches you, my mother will have passed to our Maker. Mr Scott had previously offered a teaching position for me at a local girls' school—the one I used to attend. I would have room and board and a small stipend. It is more than I had hoped for. I will take over his teaching duties there when the arrangements are finished. Perhaps on one of my days off, we may visit again one day.

Write soon. I want to know everything of America. Do they truly use slaves? Are there savages? What do they eat? Are there large cities like Bath and London?

I enjoy reading your letters, I can picture River's Bend in my mind. Does it look like this?

Sincerely,
Gwendolyn Lambert

Mr Norman, the apothecary, arrived early but proved to be of little help. He had no idea what was happening, or how to assist with her mother's attacks.

"I have heard described that *mad* patients often have a peculiar time of day, but there is no prescribed treatment aside from sedatives and restraints if violence ensues."

Gwen grew more disheartened with every word he spoke.

"At the very least we may give her some sedating drops if she becomes uncontrollable. Otherwise, it will only worsen, I'm afraid," he advised.

Gwen nodded, already accustomed to those fateful words.

"Miss Lambert, it is perhaps time you considered an institution." These dreaded words were whispered. "There is a possibility she might become violent."

"No! I promised her," Gwen said adamantly. "I will not consider it. If it becomes difficult again, I have the drops now." Any institution for which she could possibly scrape together enough money and put her mother into it would not do more than house her and lock her up. Mama would be neglected and starved, and would likely die of something more heinous and violent than that which she currently suffered.

Mr Norman looked at her with pity but nodded and left quietly.

Chapter Seven

"Mr Abbott! Mr Abbott!" a shrill voice called from a distance.

Oh, no, he thought. Mrs Bradley. He had been taking a quick dip in the river, and he seriously contemplated diving headfirst back into it to avoid his neighbour, but it was not quite dark enough.

"Yoo-hoo, Mr Abbott! Is that you over there?" Mrs Bradley's plump person had rolled out of the carriage, picked up her skirts and was hastening towards him.

Andrew quickly donned his sweat-soaked shirt. He did not mind the lady, truly. He especially did not mind the delicious food she served at her table. But he had no intention of partaking of any of her four eligible daughters.

"Mrs Bradley." He bowed regally. "To what do I owe the honour? You will excuse my appearance, I hope."

She fluttered her fan furiously and took her time averting her eyes from his drenched person. She was old enough to be his mother. He tried not to laugh.

"Oh, Mr Abbott." She swatted him with her fan. "You and your British manners."

He thought to himself ungraciously that she was not so far removed from a harpy in a country ballroom.

"We only just realized that Mr Bradley had neglected to secure you for the church bazaar. It is my dear Jenny's birthday and it is her fondest wish that you dance with her."

He hoped that he had suppressed the groan that he felt. There was no way to refuse and not sound like a cad.

"I came right over to fetch you when we realised our omission. There is also a pie contest and we need you to judge." She smiled coquettishly at him.

"How can I refuse? I will get dressed and be right over." Dared he hope there was a whisky-judging contest?

"I don't mind taking you in my carriage."

"That won't be necessary ma'am. I could not live with myself if I knew I'd caused you to miss any more of the bazaar."

"Oh, yes, indeed! You are so gentlemanly and thoughtful, Mr Abbott."

He helped her back into the carriage, resisting the urge to shove. He waved and smiled as she drove away, and looked at his porch swing longingly.

The bazaar was teeming with all the locals. He felt like a pig roasting on a spit when he walked in the door. He would give credit to his English counterparts, for they were for the most part superior in the art of subtlety. He immediately had a line of females asking him to dance. He considered himself open- minded, but this was beyond anything he had ever experienced.

He was certain the last time he had visited it had not been so *different*.

"Ah, Mr Abbott, you have arrived at last."

At last another man. "Good evening, Mr Bradley."

"I see you've already discovered our backwards bazaar. Forgive my oversight and for sending the missus to fetch you. I was preoccupied with my pie."

Backwards was one polite way to put it. "Backwards, sir?"

"We do it every year for a bit of fun. The men do the cooking, and the ladies ask the men to dance."

"You are very forward in your thinking, sir."

"Perhaps, but there is really no harm is there? Now you see why the ladies were so keen for your arrival. Can I get you a drink?"

"Much obliged, sir." *Please keep them coming.* He turned to face the crowd of hovering females and smiled.

"Who's first?"

Dearest Gwendolyn,

I attended the ladies' 'backwards bazaar' this evening. Bizarre does not begin to describe it. They have a night where the men cook, and the ladies ask the men to dance. I hope they made good money for the children's benefit; I left with bruised feet and a cracked tooth. I will say of Mr Bradley (he owns a neighbouring plantation) that he makes a delicious pecan pie (a nut that grows on trees here), but the other pies were a bit impossible to chew. I was bestowed the honour of judging duty. My neighbours are what we would call new money or, less graciously, cits.

I believe I danced every dance. Mrs Bradley saw to it that all four of her daughters were partnered with me. I cannot blame her entirely, for the unattached male crop is either overripe or under-picked. Speaking of crops, would you believe they distill rye whisky here? It is repulsive. I've almost convinced Mr Bradley to convert to barley. They say George Washington was fond of whisky, and he had a proper Scot to run his distillery. He was, however, rather a stickler about moderation. Now you will be educated in all things important for your visit here. The house is almost ready for you to paint it. Your sketch was quite good, but looks more like the Mt. Vernon estate.

Yours,

Andrew

He put down the pen and crawled into bed. Life here was not so bad,
but it was missing someone. With every decision he made about River's
Bend, he considered how Gwen would like it or what she would think.
He was pathetic, especially because his feelings were not reciprocated.
He'd hoped she might jump on a boat and follow him, but her mother
was too ill. Not that his grandmother would allow it if her mother were
not an invalid. Perhaps Miss Lambert feared she would wind up on a
deserted island or be captured by miniature people. In retrospect, his
gifts to her might not have been the wisest choice. Whatever the reason,
he needed to stop obsessing about her. It would only make it more
difficult later. But every time he closed his eyes, all he could dream
about was having her in his arms.

~*~

Had it been months since Mr Abbott left? It seemed as if it had been
some fantastic figment of her imagination, for her daily reality was such
that she was no longer certain what was real anymore. It was but a
distant memory in the quagmire in which she was now caught.

Her mother's nightly fits of confusion and agitation had worsened, and
the sedating drops worked so well that she'd become dependent upon
them. She watched her mother, who was now sleeping peacefully, and
marvelled at the change from moments before. As soon as the drops
wore off, the other person that inhabited her mother's body would
appear. She sometimes refused the drops and became more agitated and
difficult, to the point where Hettie would have to help hold her down to

get her to take them. No one should have to spend the end of their days like this.

Gwen was exhausted and feared for her own sanity. She only slept in small amounts, and even then with one eye open, too afraid of what would happen if her mother wandered away. No one else could calm Mama, even if she were to have anyone else. Hettie was not helpful, even though she meant well, but the servant had no patience for her mother in this state.

Gwen did not always have patience herself, and felt unconscionable guilt when she would snap at her mother. There were days when she did not know how much longer she could keep going like this. She constantly questioned whether she was doing the right thing. She could see her mother was dying, but she had no way to stop it. If she did not sedate her, Mama would change into an agitated aberration. She barked a mocking sound to herself. Either way you looked at it, it was brutal, she thought.

"God, if she can't be better, then please take her quickly and peacefully," Gwen whispered.

"Should we call in the doctor, Miss?" Hettie asked worriedly.

"He already said there was nothing more he could do."

"There has to be something can be done. 'Tisn't natural," Hettie tsked.

"No, it is not natural, but the doctor is out of suggestions. I'm afraid we, and she, will have to suffer through it," Gwen replied despondently.

"It can't go on forever like this. She hardly be eatin' enough for a wee one. Not that we hasn't tried. She's taken to her bed mostly, or she falls." Hettie stated the facts out loud as if it would make a difference. "You think she knows what is happenin'?"

"Sometimes she does, and that, Hettie, is the part that will forever bother me when I think of this time." It also made her have false hope when she would catch a glimpse of her mother in a seemingly normal state of mind.

"'Tis a pity." Hettie shook her head. "Such a waste."

The servant walked out still shaking her head. Gwen agreed, but she had few resources to do anything else. She wasn't sure that, were she to have all the riches in the world, anything would have been different. Sometimes things happened that there was no earthly explanation for.

Mr Abbott,

I'm sorry I have been a poor correspondent, but I have had little of note to write about. My mother is declining rapidly, and I have not left the house for weeks, if you can believe that. She is frequently out of her senses, and agitated. The doctor has prescribed calming drops, but now she has become dependent on them and sleeps the day away. If this continues, she will soon waste away.

I confess I am saddened by this change, and it is more difficult to bear without your grandmother's kindness. I look forward to your letters; they are a ray of sunshine in this dark time.

Your pitiful correspondent,

Gwen Lambert

Chapter Eight

The end had arrived quickly, yet not quickly enough. During the past few weeks Gwen had watched and waited for her mother to die. Her mother had known it was coming, Gwen had seen the terror in her eyes. That look would haunt her forever, because she hadn't been able to save her mother.

When it was finished, Gwen had been so busy making arrangements she had not had time to grasp the full reality of her situation. The solicitor had already come to call on her and inform her she had one week to leave her home. Only seven more days to pack up what was left of her life and find another situation. Days when she wanted to crawl into her bed and cry, but instead had to force herself to continue on. First, she pulled out of the attics the old mourning gowns from when her father and brother had died. She'd hoped to never see them again. Second, she wrote to the Dowager as promised.

Next, she would pay a visit to Mr Scott and accept the offer of teaching. She hoped she could make enough to find a room at a respectable boarding house for ladies, and perhaps keep Hettie, who had been with her family for as long as she could remember, and did not deserve the cruel fate of being deposited on the curb. Hettie had already done without wages for six years. Gwen had not deserved her fate either, but she could find work somehow.

She donned her darkest gown and set out for Milsom Street.

"Good morning, Mr Scott."

"Hello, Miss Lambert. Please accept my condolences for your loss."

"You have heard, then."

He nodded. "What shall you do now?"

"I was hoping the offer of teaching still stood."

He let out a small gasp of mortification.

"Oh, Miss Lambert. The position was given away not two months past. I confess, when I saw you with the London swell, I thought something finer was in the works."

Gwen blushed. "I'm afraid not, sir. Are there any students I might take on privately here?"

"I do not have any students at the moment, but I will be happy to send them your way should I hear of anyone. Shall I give them your direction?"

"I am afraid not. I must leave our current accommodation. If I stay in Bath, I shall let you know."

"I'm terribly sorry, Miss Lambert." He looked at her with deep sorrow and affection for his old pupil. "If you have any paintings you would like me to sell for you?"

"I will consider it. Thank you kindly, Mr Scott. Goodbye."

"Goodbye, Miss Lambert."

Gwen exited the shop and fought for composure. This was a heavy blow indeed. She took a deep breath. She did not have time to indulge in self-pity. She headed towards the employment agency, hoping she could find work as a companion. She was not precisely qualified to be a governess or a maid, but she was a quick study.

She was turned away kindly but promptly. The proprietress informed her that without experience or reference, she was not useful to the agency. She was too pretty to be a governess at any rate, and she would require more genteel abilities such as languages and musical talents to be sought after. The woman hinted at a career open to comely young ladies who had fallen down the ladder, and she could recommend a decent house where the girls were well fed and not beaten. How was that for a recommendation?

Gwen walked around, attempting to think of where else to look, dejected and reflecting on what the agency proprietress had said. Sadly, she realised that after a week or two of hunger and filthy accommodation, she might not be so condemning of the profession. She'd always felt sorry for the girls who had to use their bodies to survive. She would swallow her pride and beg the Dowager first if it came to that, but she would only ask if desperate.

Afterwards, she visited her old school to enquire of other teaching positions, but she had not completed her schooling and was unqualified. No, the headmistress said, she did not know of any other available positions.

As a last resort, Gwen decided to see what might be available at the nearby inn. She did not last five minutes inside whilst waiting to speak to the owner. She was immediately ogled, and when the first drunkard had pinched her bottom, she escaped before he could pinch anything else. She returned home after a long, fruitless day of searching, exhausted and discouraged.

She went up to her bed, curled up and cried. She felt alone, grieving, and for the first time, frightened for her future. Night-time was the most difficult, for she was alone with her loss. She would be overcome with sadness and tears and had to force herself to remember her mother's suffering. The passage from *Robinson Crusoe* kept repeating itself in her mind: *My heart dies within me. Alone. Forever alone.* She could not compare to being alone on an island, but for all the people surrounding her on this island, she felt so alone with no one to turn to or take care of her. It was difficult to erase her last vision of her mother when she closed her eyes. She missed her mother so desperately that she ached physically. She would give anything to have her mother back—if healthy.

The next morning, things looked slightly less grim by daylight. She decided to begin packing, knowing that leaving was becoming an inevitable reality. Going through her mother's things was a necessity—forced into grieving at the solicitor's pace instead of her own. There was little left after six years of being poor. She folded up each garment lovingly, reminding herself that her mother was no longer in pain as tears streamed down her face.

Her mother had given up her will to live. Gwen tried not to be angry at her mother for dying. Selfishly she'd wanted her to fight for her, not to abandon her! She'd stopped eating, because it was too difficult to swallow. She'd often choke, and Gwen feared she would watch her die of suffocation. She'd tried desperately to get her mother to eat, but Mrs Lambert had pushed it away or shaken her head, except for occasional sips of tea or broth.

Gwen held a momentary flash of irritation that the Dowager had also appeared to abandon her. But that was ridiculous. Neither she nor her mother were the Dowager's responsibility. However, it had cheered her mother and given her something to look forward to everyday. Gwen had not been enough. She folded the last of her garments as warm tears turned into sobs. She sat down on the empty bed in the empty room and let herself go until she had no tears left.

Hettie eventually came into the rooms and put her arms around Gwen.

"Thank you, Hettie," Gwen said as she pulled back. "I've finished here."

"And I've finished downstairs. What would you like me to do with the painting things Mr Abbott left you?"

"I will see to those. We only have the attics left, then?"

"I believe so. I'll take the things 'round to see what I can get for them when we've finished."

Gwen nodded. She rose and went to the dressing table. She'd forgotten about the small drawer. She opened it and found a small velvet purse. Though she had no hope of finding anything in it other than paste, nevertheless she pulled out a necklace from inside. It certainly looked like her mother's old pearl necklace, but that had to have been impossible given their near impoverished state. She decided to hold onto the necklace for memory's sake, and to sell it if necessary: even paste pearls might be worth something. For now, it was all she had left of her mother.

She went to the parlour, where the last things remaining were the easel, a few canvases and paints. She had a flash of a scene in her mind, and suddenly she needed to paint to release her built-up emotion. She felt mildly guilty for being so indulgent when Hettie was upstairs packing, but if her picture was decent, she would take it to Mr Scott to ask him to try and sell for her.

She stood at the easel and closed her eyes, and saw a vision of a dark, sinister sky. It came to life on the canvas before her, her heart pouring its grief out. Soon she had painted tumultuous waters beneath, and added only a small hint of colour in the sun that fell beneath the horizon, providing a counterpoint to the dark emotion, the last small ray of hope in the depths of her despair.

"Help me find that ray," she prayed. She somehow knew that she would find a way, though she had no idea how. She had to be strong. There was no one to do so for her.

She went upstairs to her room one more time, a little less emotional; perhaps she had simply become numb. Whatever the cause, she slept all night for the first time in months.

~*~

The next morning, she finished packing her small valisse. Hettie had managed to sell their belongings and delay their destitution a bit longer. Hettie was returning to live with her sister. There was no other choice. They said their tearful goodbyes, "It just don't sit right with me, leavin' you all alone, Miss Gwen," Hettie wailed.

"I am not happy to part with you, either, dearest Hettie. But there is nothing for it. My funds will go farther on my own. I'll always have the Duchess to fall back on."

With these tearful reassurances, she saw her last measure of comfort onto the stage.

After one final pass through the house, she made her way downstairs after saying her final goodbyes to the rooms she'd called home these six years past. It somehow seemed more final than when they had been forced from their manor house. She'd still had her family then. Now she had no one. The full reality of her situation still had not sunk in, even though she knew it would hit her hard, and soon.

She wished Mr Abbott was here, or that she was in America with him. She quickly pushed those thoughts aside. She missed his company, but he would have felt obligated to do something for her, just as the Dowager would. She was not their problem. She needed to try to make her own way. If that failed, and she was desperately afraid it would, she would then see if the Dowager could provide a reference and help her find a position.

She carefully wrapped the painting to be carried to Milsom Street. She looked at the easel longingly, but she would arrange for Mr Scott to pick it up and possibly sell it. She packed her remaining paints and canvases, hoping she might be able to make a little from her work until she found a permanent position. She set her valisse down, intending to return for it after the painting had been delivered.

Mr Scott had been delighted with the painting, even calling it remarkable and not commenting on her detour from her usual style. That task taken care of, she walked slowly back towards her room to fetch her bag in preparation for travelling to the boarding house.

There was a carriage in front of the building when she arrived at her rooms again. The solicitor had not wasted any time, she thought spitefully. She hoped Mr Scott would come for the easel soon. She walked to the door, and a footman nodded to her while he held the horses. She took a breath and turned the handle, hoping she at least appeared pleasant.

She did not want to speak to another soul at the moment. She wanted to be allowed to have her final moment of closure alone. Perhaps she could ask them to give her one more hour. She took a deep breath and opened the parlour door. The easel was still sitting there, as was her valisse and small trunk: her last worldly possessions. She walked further into the house and looked into the parlour. A gentleman stood there looking out of the window with his back towards her, holding an ebony malacca cane and a high-crowned beaver hat.

She did not recognise him, but his dress and his equipage proclaimed him to be of the first stare. She hesitated and cleared her throat.

He turned at the sound. "I beg your pardon. The door was unlocked."

He looked up. "Cousin Gwendolyn, is that you?" He started towards her.

"Yes, Lord Kendall." She bowed curtly. What was he doing here?

"Am I too late?" He pulled up at her cold reception.

"Too late?" She was confused. He was six years too late in her opinion.

"Your mother wrote to me of her condition. I came as soon as I received the letter. I'm afraid I only received it two days ago, though it appeared she posted it several weeks prior."

"The letter. I had not realised." Gwen had forgotten to ask to whom the letter was for. She should have paid attention. "If you came for my mother, then you are too late. She passed on seven days ago. As you can see I am closing up the rooms."

"Accept my condolences. I assumed as much with your deep mourning."

She inclined her head.

"Where do you intend to go?"

It was a natural question to ask, but she did not wish to answer it. Her pride forbade her from proclaiming her destitution and desperation, even though it was likely obvious. She did not want anyone's pity, least of all his. She blushed and turned away.

"It has not yet been decided."

"I do not pretend to deserve your forgiveness, but I ask for it anyway. I know my family behaved abominably after your father's untimely death. And when Jonathan was killed...Father forbade me from looking for you. I'd no inclination of your direction until your mother wrote to me."

He seemed sincere, but she had difficulty believing he could not have found them had he tried.

"Why don't you allow me to provide for you now?"

If he was offering another slip on the shoulder, she would find something to harm him with. She could take no more insults at the moment.

"What did you have in mind?"

"For now, I would take you to London. Mother will know what we should do."

"London?"

"Kendall House is there. I have been up north for the summer, so I did not receive your mother's letter until I returned."

"I see. I do not have a maid to travel with me. I had to turn her off."

"We may travel as brother and sister easily enough. And it is only one night to London. Your brother was my age, and we are related after all."

Gwen did not wish to go with him. She did not wish to be beholden to him. If she had any other options she would refuse. He seemed to understand this and seemed genuinely repentant.

"Will my aunt and cousins be upset by your generosity?"

"Certainly not." He dismissed the question with a wave of his hand, but did not look her in the eye. "It was all my father's doing. He was always a high stickler and overly proud of the family name."

She looked out the window and pondered in silence a few minutes. If things did not work out, she would have more options for positions. Perhaps her aunt would help her find somewhere if she arrived and was wished at Jericho, as she suspected she would be.

"Please, Cousin Gwendolyn. I owe this to Jonathan, if you will not let it be for your sake alone," Peregrine pleaded.

Her heart twisted within her chest. Jonathan would have urged her to go with him and have told her to stop letting her pride overcome her sense.

"Thank you, Cousin. I do not wish to take your charity. But you have found me at a point non plus. I have been unable to find a situation here on my own. I will accept your generosity temporarily until I may find myself something satisfactory."

He smiled broadly, revealing a handsome set of teeth. He was elegant, but she would not have thought him handsome unless he had smiled. It had changed his face and set her more at ease.

"I will have Connors load your belongings."

"May we make one stop in town? I need to deliver a message."

"Of course."

Gwen dropped off her new direction for Mr Scott in case he sold one of her paintings. She kept the easel at her cousin's insistence, and they began their journey to London.

They made a study in contrast together, Gwen reflected, as they toiled along the Bath road. He, with tasselled Hessians, shiny enough to see one's image in, a yellow-striped waistcoat to match his fitted pale yellow pantaloons, a mathematically-tied cravat, and a blue coat that moulded to his form. His eyes were as black as a moonless night, and his hair was nearly as dark with a small wave through its Brutus style. Gwen sat across from him in unrelieved black, save for her hair and eyes, in a drab crape gown, feeling like the poor relation she was.

She could not quite be comfortable despite the elegant, well-sprung carriage. She had never been around her cousin much, and she had not allowed that her brother was a good judge of character when Peregrine had broken the connection after their father's disgrace. He was of her brother's age, and they had been friends through Eton and Oxford, until Jonathan had left for the Army. Her cousin was all politeness, but she could not help but be uneasy about the welcome she would receive in London.

Chapter Nine

"Where could she have gone?" the Dowager demanded of the footmen she had sent to rescue Gwen.

"I have no idea, ma'am. I did as you 'nstructed. I drove to the address and knocked on the door, but the place was empty. I asked the neighbours, and one thought they saw'd her drive off with a gent in a fancy coach."

"Said 'er maid Hettie had gone back home to 'er sisters," the other man added.

"I cannot believe she didn't come to me," the Dowager sighed in exasperation. "Very well. I must think of what to do. You may go rest for now." She rang for her maid.

"Hanson, I need to dress to go to the court. I'd best consult the others on where to look. I'm too upset to think straight. I cannot credit that she ran away without so much as a word."

"Perhaps she wrote and you ain't received it yet," the maid suggested.

"Perhaps. She did write to me of her mother's death. What if something has happened to her? I will never forgive myself."

"No need to fret just yet, Your Grace. They'll know what to do."

The Dowager hurried uncharacteristically through her toilette in her urgency to reach counsel. She implored Hendricks to call for everyone to meet her in the parlour on a matter of the utmost importance as soon as she entered the court. She went so far as to request her grandson, Lord Fairmont, be sent for from the adjacent Loring Abbey. She paced around the parlour debating her options over and over in her mind until the family began to rush to her summons.

When everyone was present she began to recite the few facts she had at her disposal.

"Is there anyone in Bath she might have left her direction with?" Lord Easton asked.

"I would have thought she would have left it at Sir Charles's place, but she did not," the Dowager remarked with a frown.

"Is there any place she frequented? Any friends she would have informed?"

"No friends. She never left the house, except to go to the lending library."

"Did the footman say if the carriage had a crest on it?"

"No, but we could certainly ask. It would narrow the field to some extent."

"I think we should send some more men to ask around. We can also send some out to the posting inns along the main roads from Bath," Lord Easton decided.

Elly spoke up after listening thoughtfully. "I think we should try to determine what gentlemen she would have been comfortable leaving with. You said she was not the type to turn towards a less genteel occupation—"

"Certainly not!" the Dowager interrupted.

"I was going to say, what else would give her cause to leave with a gentleman?" Elly finished, unperturbed.

"She could be seeking a governess post, or even that of a companion. They could be retrieving her," Lord Fairmont said.

"I do not believe she had adequate connections to obtain such a post, but it might be worth enquiring at the employment agency in Bath. However, a gentleman would not normally go themselves to retrieve a paid servant," the Dowager replied, growing more worried.

Lord Easton rose. "I will go myself with some of the men to Bath to search immediately. I will send word if I find anything."

"Grandmamma, if you do not think she could have been hired by a gentleman, who else could it be? You said you were her last remaining family."

"That is not entirely true. I am her last relative who acknowledges her."

"I see. Do you think it possible her other relations could have come for her?"

"I think it highly unlikely. However, Millicent did remark on the connection shortly before I left. Perhaps she contacted them."

"What is the family name? I could enquire of them," Lord Fairmont offered.

"Kendall."

"I know of him. I can send an express immediately."

"If they had not been so brutal about severing the connection, I could more easily credit it. Very high in the instep the old Lord and Lady Kendall were."

"The son seems tolerable, but I hear the estates are encumbered and he shows no predilection for economy—especially at Waitier's." It was a well-known high-stakes gaming establishment in London.

"I had not heard their circumstances were precarious. It makes even less sense why they would be willing to take in a poor relation."

"Try not to fret. Adam will find something," Elly said in attempt to reassure her.

"I pray he does, or I may never forgive myself," the Dowager said in a rare display of discomposure.

~*~

96

"Mother, you remember Cousin Gwendolyn," the Viscount said when they arrived after two days on the road.

Gwen curtsied deeply, conscious of her inferior appearance in the grand townhouse. "Hello, Lady Kendall."

"Oh, child! Such formality! I will be most offended if I hear anything other than Aunt Louisa, if you please. You are very welcome." She took Gwen's hands and kissed each cheek. "I dare say you are dreadfully exhausted after your recent ordeal."

She was momentarily taken aback by the unexpected greeting. After she recovered, she said, "I am rather tired, but I am grateful for a place to put up temporarily."

"Nonsense!" Louisa waved her hand dismissively. "I won't hear of temporary. You are family, and this is where you belong. Let us allow you to rest before dinner, and we can chat when you feel more the thing."

Gwen could not have been more astonished at her reception, she reflected when finally alone. She sensed that she was expected, when all the while she had been anxious about the family's feelings at seeing her again. She had been welcomed by her aunt Louisa whom she had not seen since she was a girl some twelve years prior. She was embraced like a long-lost child and ushered upstairs to an elegant bedroom outfitted in the current mode of luxury. She had expected bare civility at best and a small room with the servants. She could not help but be suspicious.

After she had bathed and rested, a maid came to dress her for dinner. Her wardrobe was sparse, save the one gown given by the Dowager she could not bear to part with, and a few black dresses for mourning—and her mood.

She was shown downstairs to the parlour, where her aunt and cousin

Peregrine awaited her. They were joined by her other cousin, Lady Fanny, her husband Lord Dabney, and Louisa's mother, Mrs Morris. She was made known to everyone. Her cousin Fanny she'd had little acquaintance with, and while everyone was openly friendly with her, she could not feel at ease. She wished she had not come. She wished she'd had a choice.

She was escorted into dinner by her cousin Peregrine and seated next to him. A lavish dinner was placed before her, and they began to talk of her stay.

"Is this your first visit to London, Cousin Gwen?" Lady Fanny asked.

"It is."

"What do you think of our busy metropolis?" Lady Dabney asked, making small talk.

"I have yet seen very little. I confess it is much more crowded and noisy than I had imagined."

"And Town is quite empty right now!" she exclaimed.

"It is no matter. There is very little she may be permitted to do in mourning," Aunt Louisa remarked.

"Surely we may do a few things without offending the proprieties. She must have some dresses at any rate," Lady Fanny added, with an indiscreet glance at Gwen's dowdy dress.

"That will not be necessary ma'am. I do not wish to attend anything other than perhaps church. If I may take some walks in the park I believe that will satisfy me."

"I had hoped to have a few small dinner parties to introduce you. Nothing grand or inappropriate, mind you. No musicales or dancing until your mourning is lifted and you may be presented properly."

"Thank you. I hope you will not put yourself to trouble on my account, however. I do not intend to stay long. Only long enough to find an acceptable position."

"Nonsense, my dear. I will not hear of it. We have more than enough room, and are delighted to have you. Now that my Fanny is married, I will enjoy having your company. Mother does not enjoy going to balls and parties."

"Too old to give a…"

"Yes, thank you, Mother," Aunt Louisa interrupted before Mrs Morris could finish.

Gwen bit back a smile. Apparently the woman had no restraint. She watched her toss back the contents of her glass and call for another.

"I insist on presenting you when you cast off your weeds. You are still in bloom and should take nicely."

"I thank you, ma'am, but I have not a penny to rub together. I can ill afford to be presented, and would hardly be a matrimonial prize," she said frankly, knowing she was being crass.

"You shall leave that for me to worry over." Louisa reached out to pat Gwen's hand. "We have time, and you might change your mind when you become accustomed to being here."

Her tone suggested she would not argue the point, and Gwen had no intention of remaining in the house long enough to bother.

"Shall we withdraw, ladies? Perhaps, when the men join us, we could play some cards."

The women followed her aunt into the parlour, and she sat down, feeling even more out of place with Peregrine gone. She was slightly more at ease with him, and she felt somewhat sheltered from viperish tongues with a man present. Not that the ladies had given any inclination to speak of her so, but she was wary because of how her mother had been treated by them.

Aunt Louisa and Fanny began a discourse on where it would be appropriate to introduce Gwen, and all of the places she needed to be taken to be outfitted first. Gwen had no intention of being beholden to them longer than necessary. She would pretend the headache if necessary, and find her way to the employment agencies.

When the men rejoined them, she was only aware of a pressing need to be alone. She made her excuses and retired early. Once the maid had helped her into her night clothes, she sat on the window seat hugging her knees and wondered what Mr Abbott was doing in America. Was he looking at the same stars as she? The week with him seemed a distant memory. In her wildest fantasies, she had hoped he would return and come for her. For a time, it had seemed a remote possibility. Now, her hopes were fading. She had no way to send a letter to him now. Instead, she decided to pen a letter to the Dowager to let her know where she was and have her cousin frank it for her.

~*~

Andrew wiped the sweat from his brow as he heard a horse approaching. He was rarely presentable these days because he was working—and hard. They had been framing the new stables, while the masonry workers laid brick and mortar to part of the façade. He continued driving in a nail without looking to see who approached.

The horse pulled up near to him with one Miss Jenny Bradley perched atop in a plum-coloured riding habit. He looked behind her to see if she was unaccompanied. He shook his head. He remembered his sister use to ride about these parts on her own as well.

"Miss Bradley." He bowed slightly.

"Mr Abbott." She gave a nod of her head, and eyed his open shirt and rolled up sleeves with a glance beneath her hat. He was not here for social purposes, so he wasn't about to apologise to an uninvited miss. He would make certain that they were not alone together before he found himself staring down the end of her father's shotgun.

"How may I help you today, Miss Bradley?" he said in his normal cordial manner.

"Mama sent a picnic for you and your workers." She nodded to the loaded down saddlebags. "She thought you strapping young lads might be hungry," she added with a coy smile.

"Much obliged, Miss Bradley." He turned towards the men. "Abe? Would you find someone to help Miss Bradley unload her gifts in the kitchen?"

The girl looked perplexed. Obviously she had planned to unload it right there and partake of it in his company. Andrew was not keen on her plan. It was one thing to converse amiably when at her family's home for dinner. He had too much town bronze not to notice a female looking to trap him.

"But…but are you not hungry now, sir? I'd be happy to serve you."

"Not at all, ma'am. The Marshalls brought us some fresh muffins and biscuits earlier." He rubbed on his full belly to enhance the effect. His London friends would be horrified at his vulgarity, but he was desperate. "We cannot stop for a break for a few more hours. We have to get this done before the sun sets. Please send my appreciation to Mrs Bradley."

He watched the young lady stew a moment trying to forge a new plan. She was not a bad looking chit, but no one held a candle to his Gwendolyn. He had never been one for females who put themselves forward, though he really could not blame them for trying.

"Papa also invited you to come for dinner tomorrow night. He has a new home brew he wants your opinion on."

"Ah, perhaps that could be arranged. Tell him I would be delighted. Good day, Miss Bradley." He tipped his hat and turned away.

"Good day, Mr Abbott." He went back to nailing, so she reluctantly allowed Abe to lead her horse around to the kitchens. She came back by one last time when they were finished, even though it was not the direct route to the road. She waved and jumped the hedge.

"That one's going to break her neck," one of the workers remarked.

"Showing off for Mr Abbott, she was," another worker retorted.

"She can show off for me anytime."

"We're not posh enough for the likes of her," the second scoffed.

"You are both welcome to try," Andrew replied with a smile.

"You don't seem to fancy her," the workers looked at Andrew as if he was daft.

"She's well enough, I suppose, but I've got someone else in mind for the role of Mrs Abbott."

"You've got a sweetheart back home?"

"A stunning redhead," he said dreamily, before catching himself. He would regret saying that later, he was certain.

"Oh, that will make the ladies' feathers fly here. They ain't going to like that one bit."

"We won't mention it unless it becomes necessary," Andrew suggested.

"Well, that ain't right if you don't mind me saying so, sir. They've all got their hopes up, you see."

"Pardon?"

"Yes, sir. That's all they ever talks about in town."

"You'd be best off hushin' them up now."

"But it's none of their concern!" Andrew exclaimed.

"Mebbe not, but they be doin' it anyways."

Andrew hit a nail as hard as he could in frustration.

"Very well. Say what you must. I've done nothing beyond the common civilities, and I'm not about to shackle myself to any of them."

The men stared at him.

"I beg your pardon. The ways are very different here. There is nothing wrong with any of your ladies, I just never realised they were so, so...."

What could he say that would not be offensive?

"Eager?" One of the men offered.

"Precisely." Their word was much better than his choice.

"That's all right then. You leave it to us."

Chapter Ten

The Dowager was beginning to fret. She never fretted. It had been a week, and she had heard nothing. There had been no reply from Lord Kendall to Nathaniel's query. She decided to make her way back to the court to see if Easton had returned with news. What would she tell Andrew if she could not find her?

"Good morning, Grandmamma," Elly said cheerfully.

"Good morning, dear. Please tell me you've heard from your darling husband."

"Indeed. He arrived late last night and did not want to wake you. He is in his study."

Elly rose awkwardly from her chair and greeted her grandmother with a kiss on the cheek before escorting her to the study. Lord Easton looked up from his desk and smiled at the pair. He stood and came over to greet them.

"Yes, yes, good morning to you, Adam dearest. I must know what you learned," the Dowager said impatiently. The ladies sat down and he perched on the edge of the desk.

"Unfortunately, I did not find Miss Lambert. I did discover there was a crest on the carriage, but little else. None of the neighbours have any idea where she has gone."

"For shame!" the Dowager exclaimed.

"I also spoke to the employment agency. The woman finally confirmed after much coaxing that she not only told Miss Lambert she was unqualified for a governess or companion position, but she had also had the good sense to recommend a well-respected brothel to her."

"The odious mushroom! How dare her!" the Dowager cried indignantly.

"Oh, she was rather proud of herself for her charity," Adam added dryly.

"I've no doubt. Were you able to discover anything else? Nathaniel has received no response to the enquiry he sent Lord Kendall. I assume Elly filled you in on the connection?"

"She did. I had the men search the posting houses along the Bath road and confirmed Lord Kendall stayed with his *sister* in Reading the evening Miss Lambert left."

"That, we may keep to ourselves," she muttered.

"I do not understand why he has not returned Nathaniel's enquiry when they are clearly in town? It is easy enough to allay our fears," Elly remarked.

"I do not understand why they are taking her in. You may not remember their Turkish treatment after her father's death, but I do," the Dowager said, incredulous.

Sir Charles, who had joined them and was listening intently spoke. "I find it curious myself after having dealings with the old Lord and Lady Kendall. I cannot credit that Lady Kendall would suddenly change her stripes."

The Dowager stood abruptly. "That's it! I have had enough!"

"Where are you going, Grandmamma?"

"To London, of course. Something about this smells rotten and I do not intend to be fobbed off!"

~*~

A week had passed and Gwen had received no response from the Dowager. It was unlike her not to respond, but her plate must be full with her granddaughters. She was attempting to acclimate to life in a great house. The first morning she'd been awake with the servants. She was so accustomed to performing household chores and tasks that she could no longer sleep in. When the maid came to empty her chamber pot and bring fresh water she'd been startled and almost sent the maid away.

She did her best to be grateful for a roof over her head and plenty of food, but there was no affection in this house. The civilities seemed trite and insincere. The smiles they offered her never reached their eyes, and the conversations never reached beyond the superficial.

Days were quiet and filled with indolence. She did not know how to sleep until noon, have someone perform every task she was very capable of doing herself, and then be expected to spend the entire day with embroidery or chatting nonsense over tea. She did enjoy the moments of reprieve where she could lose herself in a book, but Aunt Louisa's ideas of appropriate literature did not agree with hers.

Cousin Peregrine was ever attentive, and if she did not know better, she would think he was courting her. He drove her in the park nearly every day, walked with her in the garden, and attempted to flatter her with words. She wanted to broach the topic of her finding a situation, but every mention was dismissed as ridiculous or insulting.

Gwen decided she would need to escape the house to search on her own. She had heard them speaking about making calls in the afternoon. She would excuse herself and find her way to some employment agencies. She walked towards the breakfast room, outside where she overheard her aunt Louisa speaking with Peregrine.

"How long are you going to keep the letters from her? I cannot put them off forever. It seems wrong." Her cousin's voice spoke.

"She may speak to them after you are betrothed," Aunt Louisa's voice spoke.

"She has not warmed to me, Mother. I cannot like forcing it," he complained.

"You best overcome your scruples or you will be rotting in debtor's prison. If you weren't so bacon-brained as to have gambled our fortune away, this marriage would not be necessary!" Louisa said in anger.

"I believe they would sell off my estates before it came to that," Peregrine pointed out.

"It had better not come to that," Louisa replied coldly.

"I am still to receive a nice inheritance if she marries another."

"That will barely cover the current debts. No, you must secure her hand and the entire fortune. I refuse to let this windfall out of our hands. I consider it a stroke of good luck that the idiot had enough wits left to inform us of their whereabouts. She must have forgotten about the will or her scruples. Either way, I insist you bring her up to scratch within a fortnight, or I will take matters into my own hands."

"You want me to compromise her? "

"I do. We must arrange for you to be alone with her and discovered."

"Can we not give her more time? I believe she will come around."

"We do not have the luxury of time," she reminded him.

"I refuse to go to her bedroom."

"That should not be necessary, but if it comes to it, do what you must."

Gwen knew she needed to move—that she should not be listening—but she was stunned by what she was hearing. Could they be so cold and calculating to force someone into marriage for gaming debts? It

107

frightened her to hear them speak so coldly of compromising and forcing an innocent to the altar for their gain. She had no idea they were below the hatches. They certainly did not show it with their style of living or spending habits. It sounded as if her cousin Peregrine had her father's tendency to gaming. She had heard it ran in the blood. She personally thought it showed weakness of character. A true gentleman would not put anything above his family's security.

For now, she had to find a way out of the house. She would consider the rest of their comments later. She had no intention of finding herself the next Lady Kendall, if that was even their intention. It would explain their sudden willingness to receive her and convince her of their happiness to have found her! She decided to pen another letter to the Dowager and beg for her rescue. She was not certain she knew her whereabouts after all. Upon completing this, she sneaked out of the house and made for the nearest post office.

~*~

"Well, Duchess, what a pleasant surprise!" Lady Kendall offered a polite curtsy to the Dowager and Elinor, but not without glancing at the latter's increasing belly with astonishment.

"Hello, Louisa. It has been some time. Are you acquainted with my granddaughter, Lady Easton?"

"I have not yet had the pleasure. Welcome. Please do have a seat and I will call for tea."

They uttered polite inanities until the tea tray was set before them and the Dowager could take no more of them. She had never cared for Lady Louisa Kendall, and she struggled to mask her dislike long enough to find Gwen.

"The reason I am here is that I have been informed my goddaughter is at present under your roof."

"Your goddaughter?"

"Indeed. Miss Gwendolyn Lambert. Do you deny she is here? My grandson, Lord Fairmont, sent an express enquiring after her, but it appears the messenger was detoured on his return." She raised her eyebrow in challenge.

"I had no idea Miss Lambert had any remaining connections besides our family."

"Her mother and I were cousins, and she solely charged me with her care after her unfortunate demise."

"I see. But she is of age."

"Of age, yes, and penniless. I have agreed to take her under my wing and provide her with an independence. She sent word to me, but when I sent a carriage for her, she was gone."

"Lord Kendall was informed of the situation by Mrs Lambert in a letter. He set forth as soon as he received it, but unfortunately she had already passed. He offered to provide for Miss Lambert, in fact would have done so this many years had he known where to find them."

"It was no secret. They never left Bath."

"Nevertheless, his enquiries after my husband's death went cold. He was delighted to hear from her."

"And how did you feel, Louisa?"

Elinor thought it best to intervene at this point. "May we see her? I've not yet had the pleasure of meeting her, having lived in America so long."

"I am afraid she is out at the moment, but I would be happy to tell her of your call. Are you staying at Wyndham House or Loring Place?"

"I believe I would prefer to wait. I cannot be easy until I can see her."

The Dowager did not trust Lady Kendall.

"I assure you, she was in perfect health when she left earlier," Lady Kendall said, affronted.

"When do you expect her?"

"By dinner. In fact, why not join us for dinner? We are a very dull lot, and would welcome the company."

The Dowager and Elly exchanged glances.

"Very well. We would be delighted."

"Shall we say eight o'clock? Is Lord Easton with you in town?"

"He is."

"Please extend the invitation to him as well."

"I am certain he will be delighted to accompany us. Until tonight."

The ladies parted with practiced civility, but the Dowager left two footmen to watch over the house and report Gwendolyn's return.

Reluctantly, Gwen returned to Kendall House, even though she had been gone longer than she intended, having lost her way. She had been disoriented by the congestion, noise and smells. Everything had begun to look the same as she tried to find her way back, and she finally found someone who paid her enough mind when she asked for directions. She was certain her absence had been noted by now. The butler opened the door for her before she had the chance to knock.

"Welcome, Miss Lambert. Lady Kendall is waiting for you in the parlour," he said without a trace of emotion.

"Thank you, Gates." She handed him her bonnet and pelisse, and made her way into the opulent room to greet her aunt.

"Dearest Gwen," Lady Kendall exclaimed. "I have been worried to death. Where have you been?"

"I am sorry I caused you anxiety. I only intended to catch a breath of fresh air, but I became lost."

"You should never leave the house alone! You are not in Bath any longer. Please promise you will at least take a footman if you venture out again, though Peregrine or I would be happy to escort you."

"Yes, of course. I have no desire to repeat the experience."

"Well, it appears you have come to no harm. We are to have guests for dinner, so you best go change."

"Yes, ma'am."

As soon as Gwen was out of sight, Lady Kendall sought out Peregrine in his apartments.

"It must happen tonight, or there will unlikely be another chance," she demanded, as she interrupted his nightly dressing routine.

"What has happened?" he asked, unconcerned.

"I've had a call today from the Dowager Duchess of Loring and Lady Easton."

He looked at her questioningly as if her social calls were of no consequence to him. He was consumed with his cravat and annoyingly threw off his fifth attempt at the waterfall as his valet handed him yet another rigidly starched cloth.

"She is her godmother and means to rescue her!" she said impatiently.

"No call for theatrics, Mother."

"I'm not being melodramatic," she said resentfully. "The Duchess said as much this afternoon. I was scarcely able to convince her to leave, and only by offering an invitation to dine this evening."

"You don't say. I would have let her stay."

"I could not tell her that Miss Lambert was unaccounted for, could I?"

"I suppose not," he said as he looked appreciatively at the masterpiece he had created, likely thinking he would be obliged to sacrifice his art on the altar of compromise.

"I decided it would be the perfect opportunity for you to be found in *flagrante delicto* with her dearest goddaughter. She, being a high stickler, could not do anything but insist upon a quick marriage. After all, she should be thrilled to be saved the trouble of having to be saddled with her. Not to mention, marrying her off to a lord, when I guarantee even she has no aspirations so lofty!"

"No indeed," he agreed. "How shall we arrange it, then?"

"I think I prefer to begin the evening with the entertainment. Then we won't be obliged to spend an entire evening in their wretched company."

"Doing it too brown, Mother. Easton is a right one. Dowager, too, if I recall. Very good *ton*."

"Not tonight they won't be!" she insisted.

"Perhaps not. I cannot say it is my preferred method myself. Goes against the grain."

"We have no time left for your morals, Perry. Perhaps next time you will consider these things before you sign away our fortune in vowels!" she chastised.

"Shall I take my fair cousin on a walk through the garden?" he suggested more helpfully.

"As long as you put on your show in front of the company, it matters not to me where."

"I'll do my best."

"Make sure your best leaves no room for doubt."

~*~

Andrew found himself sitting in the porch swing night after night listening to the crickets chirping and staring at the stars through the ceiling of trees. He was lonely, and spent more time than was healthy dreaming about returning to England and making a life with Gwen. Her letters had become less frequent, and he could not help but grow concerned.

They had finished the harvest, and the house restoration was coming along but the work was not yet complete. The servants were celebrating their hard work tonight, and Andrew could hear the music and smell fragrant aromas from the roasting pig. Back home, the lord of the manor put on a harvest-day celebration.

Abe and Cook had seen to everything, and Andrew wondered if he would be welcome or no. He had provided the food and the brew, of course. He stood and wandered down to the cottages out of curiosity. The music was different than what he was accustomed, but it was catchy and he found himself drawn to it.

He stood on the periphery, watching the workers perform gay dances to the tune of a fiddler and a drummer. He could not help himself from tapping along and smiling. The dances were full of life and fun, not a rigid ritual of steps as Society dances were.

Abe caught sight of him and waved him over.

"Good evening, Master Abbott."

"Good evening, Abe. Am I intruding?"

"Not at all, sir."

"What are the dances called?"

"This one is a reel. The others jigs."

"I am glad to see everyone enjoying themselves."

"It was good of you to come."

Abe's young daughter ran up and stood smiling shyly at Andrew from behind her father. The shyness did not last long.

"This is my Harriet."

Andrew bowed to the pretty young girl of perhaps twelve years. "May I have the next dance, Miss Harriet?"

She looked with large eyes towards her father. He nodded.

Andrew held out his arm. "I must warn you, I have no idea how to dance a reel or jig."

The girl giggled. "I can show you how to go on. It is simple."

Soon Andrew was keeping time with the rest. "I cannot remember ever having this much fun, Miss Harriet. I must thank you for the honour of dancing with you." He bowed and escorted her back to her father who was grinning.

"Will you introduce me to some of your friends, Harriet? I find I am sadly lacking acquaintances."

"Certainly Mr Abbott."

Andrew immediately found himself with more little girls to dance with than he ever bargained for. He was old enough to be their father, and felt the first paternal inclination he had ever had. As the night wore on, the younger girls were sent to their beds and his dancing partners advanced in age. He was only able to coax Cook out of her chair for one jig, protesting yet preening from the honour he bestowed upon her.

He returned Cook to her chair and went to the refreshment table for a drink. He found himself standing next to a beautiful young lady with much lighter skin than the other servants. He had heard these interracials were often to be found on manors where owners took advantage of their servants, but he was astonished to find one on his father's property. His father was adamantly opposed to that type of behaviour.

He had heard the children of such liaisons were often shunned amongst both communities and he felt sorry for the girl. He imagined it was difficult to be caught between two worlds, and even more so with her beauty.

"I'm Andrew Abbott. He said with a friendly smile."

"I know who you are, sir. I'm Sally Cooper."

"Do you work here?"

"Yes. I'm newly come from Williamsburg. My husband died recently, and I was hired here."

"You are free, then?"

"I was freed when my husband purchased me for marriage. He survived the war, and was killed in a fight defending my honour."

"I am sorry for your loss. I was also a soldier."

She nodded and averted her eyes.

"Are you finding River's Bend comfortable?"

"Yes. Only the others do not know what to think of me. "

"They will learn over time."

"Are you lonely?"

"Sometimes."

"I am lonely." She looked at him boldly, offering herself with her eyes.

"My heart belongs to another, Mrs Cooper," he said kindly, without any rebuke.

"It was not my heart I offered," she said quietly.

"My heart and body are offered together."

"She is a fortunate woman," she said, surprised at the refusal. "You are a rare find, Mr Abbott."

She walked off quietly. As Andrew watched her walk away, Abe was suddenly next to him.

"I'd beware of that one, Master Abbott. She is a good enough worker, but was married to a white man. Not that it is any of my business, I don't want no trouble for you."

"I don't anticipate any trouble, Abe. Try to be kind to her. It must be difficult for her."

"Aye. That I always does, Master Abbott."

~*~

The ride back to Wyndham House was short, and the Dowager was in high dudgeon, most unhappy to have left the house without Miss Lambert.

"I cannot believe the nerve of that woman. Acting as if they would have welcomed Millicent and Gwendolyn into their ever-loving bosom had they been able to find them!"

"I cannot like Lady Kendall either. She made my skin crawl, but then I have never been one for the polite ways," Elly commented, her face wrinkled with distaste.

"I'd wager my firstborn they never lifted a scrawny finger to look for them!"

"I'm certain Uncle would be happy to hear it," Elly retorted.

"If you knew the lengths she went to shun Millicent and to make sure the world knew they had repudiated them, you would likely have rung a peal over her. I would like to point out that I showed enormous restraint."

"There is still dinner," Elly pointed out helpfully. "Why did you?"

"I am certain I will once I have Gwen. I will be happy to serve her a dish of her own sauce when I know Gwen is safe."

"This should make for a delightful evening."

"Quite."

"Is Miss Lambert your goddaughter? I had no idea."

"No. But she might as well be. I did agree to care for her." She waved her hand. "It is the same thing."

"Grandmamma. You are too bad!" Elly chastised with a smile.

"I have as much right to her as they do. More, in fact. I refuse to feel guilty."

"I do not expect it of you. What do you think they are planning?"

"I wish I knew. But my instinct tells me to remove her from their presence as fast as may be done."

"Do you think she will try to convince Miss Lambert to stay?"

"That depends on what they have in mind. I only wish I knew what that might be, but be certain she would not have Gwendolyn under her roof unless she stood to gain something from it."

The ladies only had time to ready themselves for dinner, having stayed well past the normal calling hours. The Dowager was waiting in the carriage for Easton and Elly to depart.

"Have you been waiting long, Grandmamma?"

"No, but I want to be there."

"Then let us go," Lord Easton said as he signalled the driver with a double tap on the roof.

They were shown into the drawing room where they were received by Lady Kendall.

"Where is she?" the Dowager demanded as soon as brief greetings were made.

Elly put her hand on her arm to calm her. "I am certain she will be down directly."

But she wasn't. Ten minutes later, Lady Kendall excused herself to ask after her son and Miss Lambert.

"For I know they are both here and went up to dress. They came in from an outing as soon as you left. It is not like either of them to be late."

Lady Kendall opened the door and asked the butler to enquire of her son and niece.

The butler commented in a calm voice, "I believe I saw the pair go into the garden, milady."

"The garden? Whatever could they be doing there at this hour?" She immediately strolled over to the doors that opened onto the terrace and pulled them wide. There for all to see was Lord Kendall awkwardly attempting to embrace his cousin.

"Well, I never! How could you, Perry?" Lady Kendall shrieked.

Lord Kendall immediately dropped his attempt at amour, and Gwen indignantly punched her cousin straight in the gut, gaining a loud "umph" from Peregrine.

"I thought females slapped you when they were angry!" he protested from a doubled-over position.

The Dowager began clapping. "Bravo Gwen! It won't fadge, Louisa. That is the worst attempt at compromising someone I've ever witnessed. It's a pity it was wasted on me. I dearly hope the pair of you never has to turn to the stage."

Lady Kendall was too stunned by the Dowager's response to recover quickly.

"Come, dearest Gwen. Let us excuse ourselves. I believe we have had our fill already."

"But she is ruined!" Lady Kendall insisted.

"I did offer her marriage before I compromised her." Even Lord Kendall was not convinced.

"Is this true?" the Dowager said with surprise.

Gwen nodded.

"Did you accept?" she asked in disbelief.

She shook her head. "No."

"Thank God," she said casting her eyes upward.

"The only thing ruined is your cravat, Lord Kendall," Lord Easton remarked, realising that travesty likely to worry this pink of the ton more than being called out.

"I saw nothing but a cousinly embrace," Elly added.

"I will be taking Gwen home with me," the Dowager pronounced as she took Gwen's hand and walked towards the door.

"Wait!" Lady Kendall called after them, but they did not stop.

Chapter Eleven

Gwen could not speak when they entered the carriage, or she would embarrass herself. The strings of words entering her mind were not ones a lady could speak; she was livid. She should have trusted her instincts and known that her father's family would not have welcomed her with opens arms unless there was an ulterior motive. She still was not certain how it would benefit them, but she wanted no part of it. The offer of marriage had shocked her. She suspected he must need to marry for an inheritance and no one else would have him. A gentleman would have taken no for an answer. Thankfully, the Dowager had put a stop to his attentions before they became irreversible. How could you offer marriage to someone, yet treat them like a light-skirt?

She was indebted to the Dowager and the Eastons; she would make a fool of herself if she attempted to express her gratitude at the moment, but what must they think of her? Her fretting was interrupted by a kind voice.

"It is a pleasure to meet you Miss Lambert," Lady Easton reached over and took her hand.

"I apologise for the unconventional greeting, Lord and Lady Easton," Gwen remarked.

"It was hardly your doing. He deserved to be called out," Lord Easton replied.

"Oh, thank goodness you did not! I could not live with that on my conscience!" Gwen exclaimed.

"I do not believe in settling matters that way, so you may be easy," Lord Easton reassured.

"I am glad to hear it. I think it an abominable practice."

"I agree wholeheartedly. A good bout of fisticuffs would cure most disputes," Lady Easton proffered her opinion shockingly.

Gwen smiled despite herself. "Lady Easton's rules for world diplomacy," she suggested.

She laughed. "Oh, please call me Elly. Everyone does. I am too familiar for England. Six years in America does not wear off overnight." She laughed and instantly Gwen felt more at ease. "Forgive me. We are terribly sorry for your loss and for the shabby treatment your cousin has offered you under his own roof. You are very welcome to stay with us as long as you please."

"Thank you. I am already indebted to you."

They arrived at Wyndham House and she was led gently upstairs by the Dowager. "If you wish to talk about anything, I am in the room two doors along."

Gwen cast her a grateful smile and nodded. "Thank you. I shall be fine presently."

"I have no doubt. There is nothing so odious as being forced to discuss one's troubles when all one wishes is the counsel of a glass of wine and a bath."

"I am sorry for the trouble I caused, ma'am."

"There is no need for apologies. I am only grateful to have found you in time." She embraced Gwen with a meaningful hug, who had to struggle with herself to not crush the Dowager. She'd had no human touch, save one hug from Hettie, since her mother had died, a time when she had needed it most. The Dowager seemed to understand and held her longer than necessary. Gwen reluctantly pulled away and said goodnight.

She undressed and relaxed into a warm bath, but barely kept her eyes open long enough to crawl into the luxurious bed. She had not slept well the entire time at Kendall House. Here, she was instantly at ease and fell into a peaceful sleep.

~*~

The Dowager, having passed a restless night concerning herself over the latest turn of events, had given up on repose and was the first to the breakfast room. She was joined shortly by Easton and Elinor, who had been unable to sleep well due to her advancing pregnancy.

"Good morning, Grandmamma. You look fagged to death."

"Very gracious of you to mention it, dear."

"What troubles you?"

"I am concerned about Gwen."

"She seemed pretty well able to care of herself. She has a handy right," Easton said appreciatively.

"Instinct tells me we have not seen the last of Lord Kendall," the Dowager said with a deep crease in her brow.

"Miss Lambert is exquisite. He was likely attempting to beat the other bachelors to the punch," Elly suggested.

"No," Lord Easton said shaking his head. "Not Kendall. A beautiful girl without fortune would only tempt him to make a backhanded offer."

"Precisely," the Dowager agreed. "There has to be more to the story than meets the eye."

"I think it might be worthwhile to visit the Kendall family solicitor," Easton announced.

"Do you think he will speak to you?" Elly asked doubtfully.

"If he wishes to maintain the Trowbridge family business, he will. Besides, I only intend to enquire after Miss Lambert's part in this. If it does not affect her, we can be off to Sussex today and not be obliged to worry."

"That is a stroke of good fortune," Elly remarked.

"I'd rather be fortunate than good," the Dowager said.

"It certainly gives us half a chance." Easton stood and kissed his wife affectionately, and made his way to visit the solicitor.

~*~

When Gwen awoke the next morning, the household was bustling with preparations to return to Sussex. She had not slept this long in years. The Eastons and the Dowager had only come to London to search for her, the maid had said. A pang of guilt washed over her. She'd never meant to trouble any of them.

She had not realised the obligation the Dowager felt to her mother, or that she would care enough to come searching for her. Gwen had thought she was doing everyone a favour by going with her cousin, who should have been the one to provide for her.

She had a roll and chocolate in her room, and hurried to ready herself so they would not be obliged to wait for her. When she arrived, the family had finished breakfasting and had returned upstairs. She went into the parlour to wait for them.

She had been too overwhelmed to notice her surroundings last night. The house enjoyed a lovely view over Grosvenor Square, and was much quieter than she had expected a London home to be. She enjoyed watching a pair of starlings chase each other about and did not notice the butler enter until he startled her by calling her name.

"Miss Lambert?"

"Yes?"

"There is a gentleman here to see you."

"Me?" she said with surprise.

Before the butler had been able to utter her visitors name, her cousin Peregrine entered the room.

"Lord Kendall, miss," he muttered sarcastically and exited, leaving the door open.

She felt a moment's panic, but hoped the butler had the wherewithal to inform Her Grace of the uninvited guest. This was not the fashionable hour for calls, and there could be no good reason for his visit.

"Lord Kendall."

"Cousin Gwen. I've come to beg your pardon."

"Very well. Good day," she said curtly.

"Pray tell why my offer was so repulsive to you? Most in your position would jump at the chance to be a viscountess. I found you penniless and offered you a home. We got on well this past week, I thought we should deal rather nicely together."

"I'm flattered you condescended to make me such an estimable offer, but I cannot imagine how a match with myself would help your situation in the least. As you said, I'm quite penniless. I haven't a single feather to fly with."

"My situation? Whatever can you mean? You cannot have considered the advantages you would have as Lady Kendall."

"I am certain there is someone out there who will be able to appreciate all your position has to offer, but it will not be me."

She saw the flash of indignation in his eyes, though he kept his face impassive. He walked over and looked out the window with his hands behind his back. She remained silent and watched him wearily.

"Very well, Cousin. You have discovered me. I must marry in order to obtain my inheritance. My father's debts have left me encumbered, and I will be forced to sell off our unentailed properties if I do not marry quickly."

"Why must it be me?"

"Why not? It seemed a perfect solution when I found you again. My inheritance makes who I marry unimportant. You are of good birth. And, I must admit, I find you a much more desirable companion than the other marriageable misses."

"It is rather sudden." She had not expected him to be so forthright with her about the circumstances. Her aunt Louisa had been convinced his gambling was the culprit. Her heart and mind warred with each other: romanticism versus ration.

"I had hoped you would warm to my suit, I admit, but many marriages are built on less connection than ours. Perhaps one day you will return my feelings."

"Feelings?" she said doubtfully.

"You must know you are a beautiful woman."

She stared at him blankly.

"Take a few days to think on it. I will not rush you more than necessity demands, but I must have an answer by the end of the week."

He took her hands and kissed them then left her standing in stunned astonishment.

"Who was that?" the Dowager entered the room as the front door was closing.

"Lord Kendall."

"The nerve of him to show his face! I never dreamt he would come, or I would have had Barnes bar the door to him!"

"He came to beg my pardon and explain himself."

"He did, did he? What did he have to say to excuse his behavior?"

"He confessed he must marry to gain his inheritance. He thought it might as well be me. He showed great condescension to bestow a favour on me, I'm sure."

"Nothing like a hefty dose of flattery to convince you!"

"I believe he thought I could not resist the opportunity to become a viscountess."

"It is an enviable position in Society," the Dowager reasoned.

"Yes, but…" Gwen hesitated.

"But?" the Dowager prodded.

"I overheard some information I should not have," Gwen said feeling a twinge of guilt.

"The best kind," the Dowager said encouragingly.

"Lady Kendall was scolding him for gaming their fortune away. He mentioned receiving a tidy sum if he married, but Lady Kendall said he must marry 'her' for the entire fortune."

"Interesting. And you do not believe this could be you?"

"I've never heard my name attached to fortune of any sort. Though we never spoke of the Kendall family after Father died."

"The old Lord Kendall would never have left you a penny," she said scathingly.

"I agree. I can make no sense of it."

"Nevertheless, Peregrine is keen to marry you. If he is desperate for funds, he will not be patient for long," she warned.

"He said I must give him an answer by the end of the week," Gwen added with a worried frown.

"Then we shall contrive make it inconvenient for him to be answered."

~*~

Andrew soon discovered there were still divided political associations in the new America since he had last visited. He had every wish to avoid anything political, but one could only decline so many invitations and not appear uncivil. His neighbours had taken the more rigid American stance, donning only Virginia homespun dresses and suits to declare their loyalty. When he had mentioned attending the British ball, he had received an oratory of their thoughts on the mother country. He assumed they had only befriended him in hopes to convert him to their way of thinking. He bore their views no ill will, but did not wish to be subjected to or prostheletised to about them. They had been born and raised here; he felt the same loyalty to England, and was thankful for a topic to provide some distance between the overly friendly family.

It seemed to Andrew as he stood in wait amongst the carriages to enter the current British Minister's residence, that Society here had evolved into something akin to mimicry of England. It was not the same, nor could it be in such a large country, but each city seemed to have developed its own hierarchy.

It seemed ironic after the fierce determination to be free from their feelings of tyranny, that the wealthy landowners were little different than the peerage. True, birth was the operative difference, but it seemed human nature ordered themselves regardless.

The new Minister, another Sir Charles, who had replaced his father, had been a friend at Oxford. His wife, Lady Mary Charlotte, was niece to the Duke of Wellington. They were having the annual ball, and had naturally extended Andrew an invitation. He greeted Sir Charles and Lady Bagot, and was shown into his father's old home. Little had changed, save a few trinkets, pictures and furnishings. Elly would be pleased to know the gardens were still cared for in a fastidious manner.

Andrew sat near Lady Bagot during dinner and compared American society to that of England. It was only natural, and she had only been in residence a year.

"What do you think of America, Lady Bagot?"

"Washington is a pleasant city. Not as large as London, of course. I do enjoy the warmer climate."

"Do you find it difficult after the recent war?"

"There are those who look down upon us, but most treat us with ambivalence or friendliness."

"There is much to be said for ambivalence."

"Indeed. I find it a most welcome virtue." She smiled with a twinkle in her eyes.

"I wish my nearest neighbours were familiar with the notion."

"They are of the overly friendly variety, I gather?"

"They could certainly stand to be taught a few things about discretion. They are cordial to me, don't misunderstand," he confided with a faint smile.

"I do not misunderstand."

"Gran would call them vulgar mushrooms," he said candidly.

She placed a friendly hand on his arm. "A handsome young man of fortune and ease is attractive, no matter. I have no doubt were you to see them in one of these settings their behaviour would be improved."

"Doubtful, but perhaps they are more comfortable with me in their home. I confess I feel like I'm being circled by vultures with their four single daughters."

"You poor thing. Should I visit and give them a set down?"

"If I thought it would do any good, dear lady, I would have asked you to do so many weeks ago!"

She laughed. "If you decide to entertain while you are here, I must be

128

so vulgar as to request an invitation. I must see these neighbours for myself."

"Consider the invitation yours. At the moment, you would be obliged to eat in the kitchen, or amongst sawdust."

"I believe I can control my urges until the house is finished." Her lips twitched. "The Americans do work hard to distinguish themselves, like our cits. If you are able to watch their dance steps, I've heard tell they measure their good breeding by their elegance on the dance floor."

"No!"

She nodded. "With their lands being further apart, there is less chance for women and men to socialise. They meet at subscription balls similar to Almack's, but political ideas are exchanged more than pedigrees. Blood lines being unimportant here."

"Wealth certainly is."

"Indeed. Even the idiot knows he cannot succeed without wealth."

"No, but the idiot will try," he said dryly.

"Shall you save a dance for me? I need to measure my political worth with my minuet."

"By all means! I had not thought you a politician," she sallied.

"Not I. But I cannot resist knowing how I measure up!"

"I shall enjoy that. If I recall, you were one of the Beau's best dancers. He never could abide anyone that could not dance."

"Not a bit. He fired more than one officer for their clumsiness." He laughed.

"Do you return to England soon? I confess I was surprised to hear you have been amongst us so long."

"I would like to be on the next boat. But I promised Father I would finish the restoration," he said with longing in his voice.

"Why the hurry?" She raised a knowing eyebrow.

He smiled a cheeky grin.

"The smile says it all. I will wish you and the lucky lady happiness now." She raised her glass.

"Thank you, ma'am." Now to convince Miss Lambert.

Chapter Twelve

Gwen and the Dowager arrived in Sussex and were driven through a grand ducal estate before arriving at the Dower House. Lord and Lady Easton had stayed in town on some urgent matter and were to follow as soon as they could. Gwen had considered her options *ad nauseum* on their journey, from running away to America, to finding a position, to accepting her cousin's proposal. There were worse fates. But she still held out the smallest piece of hope that Mr Abbott would return; she no longer fitted into society, nor cared to. She should not be thinking of him. It was somehow different to dream of a fictional character in a book. But Mr Abbott was real. A living, breathing, in-the-flesh male. He was much more threatening than any of her heroes from the page, and quite beyond her touch.

Her cousin was a Society beau, and would expect her to do him credit. She would fail miserably in his world. It was odd that she did not think her cousin so much beyond her touch as out of her realm. A realm that she was content to never enter.

She still had misgivings about taking the Dowager's charity. She did not want to be a burden or feel indebted. She could not overcome her pride in her self-sufficiency from years of independence. She had come to terms with her new position in society, and she realised she would need help to find a respectable situation, which seemed to be the best choice. She forced her feelings of anger towards her father to the back of her mind. It seemed a lifetime ago that she had lived on a sizable estate, with dreams of a season and a love match.

Her aspirations at this point were minimal: to find a kind employer, and have a warm bed and meal every day. That wasn't entirely true, she confessed to herself; she also selfishly wanted a blue-eyed charmer with a roguish smile who was currently away in America. If she had money she would be tempted to purchase a ticket for the next boat there. Talk about wanton! She doubted he would shut the door in her face if she were to show up unattended, but he might assume she was open to a different type of arrangement. This was a case where it would be preferable to be a man. She would not hesitate to leave and start a new life if she were not limited by female restrictions and proprieties.

The footman was opening the carriage door and handing her down as she dismissed her adventurous thoughts. She had no money to even dream of such things. She paused and looked around. She could smell salty air brought in by a cool breeze. Perhaps they were close to the sea as she had heard it described. It was possible in Sussex. She had never seen the sea, except for in paintings, and she suddenly felt a rush of anticipation. She would enjoy her brief foray into freedom, but only long enough to find a good position. She knew the Dowager would object, but she would have to make her understand.

Before she knew what was happening, she'd been ushered up the stairs into a fine bedroom, and was being dressed in a fine gown and her hair tamed by Hanson, Her Grace's maid.

"We don't have time for a fancy style this evening, miss. But I think this will do for now."

Gwen turned around to look and saw she has been transformed yet again. Only this time Mr Abbott would not be there to appreciate it. Stupid, *stupid* girl, she berated herself. She had to stop thinking such thoughts of him. It was going to be difficult to remember who and what her circumstances were whilst staying with the Dowager. She would have to move quickly with her search, though it hurt her heart.

When she was ready, she escorted the Dowager on a short walk to Wyndham. Dusk was beginning to fall, but she could see water in the distance. She paused and inhaled a deep breath, luxuriating in her first view of the Channel. She could not wait to explore in the morning. She thought of Mr Abbott out on a ship and the sea, and suppressed a chuckle. She could just imagine him clinging to the sides as he had vividly described.

They were shown into the mansion, and then to the drawing room where a crowd of strangers awaited her.

"Let me introduce you to everyone. We do not expect you to remember names on the first day."

She was introduced to Sir Charles, Lady Abernathy, and Lord and Lady Fairmont, and all were equally friendly. How fortunate Mr Abbott was to have a family such as this. Now she understood his mannerisms better. What she did not understand was why he had not yet married. Perhaps he was not in want of a wife. She smiled inwardly at the first line of genius from *Pride and Prejudice*. She would dearly love to take tea with that authoress one day!

"Did you have a pleasant journey?" Lady Fairmont asked.

"It was lovely," Gwen said dreamily.

"Lovely? You must have taken a new road," Lady Fairmont said doubtfully.

"Besides this trip to London, I have never been out of Bath, so anywhere is lovely to me."

"Never left Bath? You must remain in our company then, for we never stay put long. Between America, Scotland, France...you are certain to find plenty of adventure with us."

Lady Fairmont had no idea how she longed to do just that. They instantly treated her as if she were one of the family, with a genuine kindness which could not be feigned. She felt her throat tighten and water began to form in her eyes. She forced a smile and looked away. She was saved from betraying her emotion by the butler announcing dinner.

She had never experienced such a dinner. These families were obviously close and informal, which helped to put her at ease. They spoke across the table and laughed jovially, unafraid to tease one another. Lady Fairmont informed her that the men had all grown up with one another, and had gone off to the Army together as well. Lord Fairmont's sister, Beatrice, had married their other friend, Lord Vernon, but they spent most of their time in France now. The only one that did not seem happy was Lady Abernathy. She had a look of sadness about her. Gwen remembered Mr Abbott speaking of his sister, Sarah, but had said little else about her. She wished Mr Abbott was there. She would love to see him interacting with his family, and to know him better. She had only ever been with him alone, or with the Dowager.

"You are to stay with us permanently, then?" Lady Fairmont asked and smiled kindly. "I assure you, we do behave properly when we must."

"No, Lady Fairmont. I had hoped to seek the Dowager's help in finding a position."

Gwen heard a *harrumph* from across the table where the Dowager sat.

"I will not consider discussing any such thing now." The Dowager threw her chin back and turned away.

Gwen's mouth gaped, and she heard suppressed laughter and snickers from around her.

"Don't mind her, Miss Lambert. She is only teasing you. That is her way of showing affection."

Gwen tried to offer a slight smile. She had not expected such a reaction.

"You will grow accustomed to her ways," Lady Fairmont remarked with a twinkle in her eye.

"Has anyone heard from Andrew?" Lord Fairmont asked.

Sir Charles, a pleasant older gentleman with an easy smile, spoke up, "I had a letter from him yesterday. It seems he has more work than he anticipated. He is having difficulty finding a steward that he trusts to treat the workers properly."

Gwen wished she had received a letter. It had been some time since she had written herself. It took a month to send correspondence and she hadn't had the luxury of being able to post from London.

"I wonder how things have changed since we left," Sir Charles said thoughtfully.

"Perhaps someone here would be willing to take it on – start a new life there," Lord Wyndham suggested, a kind, frail man.

"Yes, many of our veterans are improved enough that they could handle such a task," Lord Fairmont said enthusiastically.

"An excellent idea!" Sir Charles agreed. "I've little doubt there is plenty of work for anyone who is interested."

"It is settled then. I shall propose it to those suited in the morning and make arrangements if any are willing."

"Andrew may have more help than he bargained for," Lord Fairmont said humorously.

"Is there any need for a housekeeper there?" Gwendolyn asked somewhat timidly.

"Perhaps. Do you know of someone?" Sir Charles asked eagerly.

She blushed. "I was thinking of myself, sir."

"Nonsense, Gwendolyn! Utter nonsense. Let us speak of something else before she gets any more nonsensical ideas into her head," the Dowager said with vehemence.

"Your Grace, I must find a position soon. And I have always longed to travel."

"Then we shall find a way for you to travel. But I will not hear of you going into service. I promised your dear mother I would see you *situated* properly."

Gwendolyn ceased speaking about it for now. She could see she would get nowhere with the Dowager.

Sir Charles and Lord Fairmont were discussing who would make a good steward for the plantation.

Gwen became absorbed and fascinated with the discussion of the homes that had been set up to help the less fortunate orphans and veterans on the estate.

As the ladies were withdrawing, a carriage pulled up bringing Lord and Lady Easton home. Everyone gathered in the drawing room to greet them.

"I hope you do not mind, but Hendricks, would you please have a small dinner set for us in here? Lady Easton is famished."

"I must defend my husband," Elly spoke up. "He offered to stop several times, but I insisted we travel on."

"We can return to the dining room, so you may be comfortable," Lady Fairmont offered.

"That is not necessary. We do wish to speak with Miss Lambert."

Gwen was about to retire and leave the family to speak in private. Lady

Abernathy excused herself, but the others remained.

"Do you wish us to leave?" Lord Fairmont asked. "I would not intrude on something personal."

"I cannot imagine anything about me that is not already known," Gwen said frankly.

"Very well," Lord Easton began. "I went to see Lord Kendall's solicitor, who also happens to be my solicitor."

Gwen creased her brow and wondered how it would concern her. She waited for Lord Easton to continue.

"Unfortunately, I wasn't unable to see him. But his clerk did inform me that when your grandfather died, Miss Lambert, there was an inheritance tied to your marriage."

"My marriage? I had no idea," she said, astonished.

"I was unable to obtain the specifics, but I left request to speak to my solicitor as soon as can be arranged."

"Thank you, Lord Easton. It had not occurred to me to do such a thing."

"I hate to raise your hopes about a dowry. The will could state you must marry your cousin in order to inherit. I have seen it done before."

"It would explain Peregrine's sudden interest. Has the family been in financial trouble for some time?"

"I have only heard about recent losses at the tables," Lord Fairmont said.

"If you wish to reconsider, we will try to help," Lord Easton said. "It would not be a terrible match for you. The family is old and well-respected, even if the last generation's collars were over-starched."

"It most certainly would be a terrible match!" The Dowager, who had been listening intently, finally spoke up. "You do not wish for it, do you,

Gwen?"

"I am uncertain." She looked down at her hands. "I have been thinking on it. Perhaps I should swallow my pride. I might not receive a better offer."

~*~

Gwen was awake at her usual early hour after having spent a restless night in thought about her predicament. She dressed and decided to explore the grounds before the household awoke. She chose the pathway they had used the night before to walk towards the sea. She had been reassured by the Eastons that she was welcome anywhere. As she got closer to the water, the winds grew stronger and blew her bonnet off. It was quite a climb to the edge, but the view was beyond imagination. Her artist's eye soaked in the beauty of the chalk cliffs and the sun on the horizon shining its glory across the ripples in the water. Her favourite part was the brilliant patterns the waves made against the rocks. She closed her eyes in an attempt to capture the moment for later, wondering if it was possible to accurately portray the spray that the waves made. She wished she had brought along her sketching paper, but she dare not return to retrieve it or she would miss the moment. She inhaled deeply of the ocean breeze, and savoured the glorious feeling.

"I see you have found our favourite spot as well," Lord Easton remarked.

"Good morning, Lord and Lady Easton." The couple were holding hands, clearly enjoying some quiet time together.

"I beg your pardon, I did not mean to intrude."

"Nonsense!" They both dismissed her objections. "We are happy you appreciate our view. We think it the finest in England."

"It would make a lovely painting," Gwen said enthusiastically.

"Are you are an artist?" Lord Easton asked.

"I used to fancy myself one, but it is more of a luxurious extravagance now."

"We would both dearly love to capture this," Lord Easton swept his hand out towards the sunrise, the water and the cliffs. "If I may be so forward as to request you to paint it for us? We have been discussing finding someone to capture its beauty for years."

"I would be delighted. I only hope I may do it justice," Gwen said modestly.

"I am certain you will. I have heard you worked wonders with Bath stone," Lady Easton chuckled.

"I have a meeting to attend this morning, if you will excuse me, ladies. Miss Lambert, may I trust you to ensure Lady Easton returns to the house before long? She tends to think her condition does not warrant special attention."

"I am not certain anyone can make Lady Easton do anything," Gwen said. "But I will do my best, sir."

They all laughed. "We shall get along famously, Miss Lambert. Come, let me show you around and introduce you to everyone. I am a bit biased and proud of course, but I do not think you will find a finer school in all of Britain."

"What made you want to open this school, if you don't mind my asking?"

"Lord Easton already had an orphanage, and he had begun the idea of schooling the orphans to train them for useful work. They don't remain children for long, and those that have no training often are taken to be chimney sweeps or other unsavoury occupations."

"Such as the workhouses." Gwen knew that to be true. She had seen it before, and had worried often that she would wind up there herself.

"Indeed. The medical training was my idea, I confess. I became rather attached to the art of medicine when I was in America. It began with helping wounded soldiers and grew from there."

"Are you a physician?" Gwen asked Lady Easton with surprise.

"Oh, nothing so glamorous, I'm afraid. I am a mere amateur. We have Dr McGinnis in charge of the school, and Josie and I help out a little. And we have Dr Craig here from Scotland from time to time. We are attempting to convince him to join us here permanently."

"It sounds like quite a venture."

"We have only been operating about three years, but I would like to think we have helped improve medicine in hospitals and in the Army."

"And what about the veterans?"

"The ones that are able are trained to help in the breeding stables, or are placed on estates with people who we trust to treat them right. Sadly, there are many that will never recover. They are given as comfortable a home as we can provide them with, and they have all the medical care they need at their doorstep."

"It seems you have thought of everything."

"Unlikely, but we do what we can. We feel it is our privilege to take care of others who have fallen on hard times, or who cannot help themselves. None of the people here chose this path."

"No," Gwen agreed quietly. She had not chosen her path either, but she would do her best to make the most of her abilities.

"Here is the good Dr Craig now. Dr Craig, may I present to you Miss Gwendolyn Lambert."

"A pleasure to meet you, lass." He proffered an elegant bow and she gave a slight curtsy. He was an extraordinarily handsome man, with deep blue eyes and a Scottish brogue. If her heart weren't in America, it would be awakened by his surplus charms.

"Miss Lambert's mother was Grandmother's cousin."

"May I offer my condolences, lass."

"Thank you, sir."

"I was showing her around the school. Are you teaching anything of interest today?"

"It is almost time for seminar. I find it interesting, but I am not certain if Miss Lambert would find it so.

"Seminar is the time of day when the students read an essay or journal piece and discuss it," Elly explained.

"A compelling essay on shaking palsies was recently published by James Parkinson, a surgeon in London. We have two veterans with similar symptoms as he describes, so I thought it an appropriate topic."

"This shaking palsy; is it when the person's body shakes?" Gwen asked.

"Sometimes it is the entire body, sometimes it is only an arm or hand."

"My mother had shaking. It was not her only problem, but her doctor did not understand what was happening to her."

"Would you like to sit in our seminar? I would love to speak to you more about your mother's condition as well."

"Of course." She looked towards Elly. "Would you mind?"

"Not at all. In fact, I would be delighted. It is time I checked on the children anyway."

"This way." Dr Craig placed one hand on Gwen's back, and the other was held out to show her the way.

~*~

Elly watched them walk away, and could not help but wonder if the two would suit. She knew Miss Lambert and her brother had become acquainted, but Andrew never seemed interested in marriage, despite all the females making cakes of themselves over him. He had written of meeting Miss Lambert and their painting escapade, but surely he would not have left for America if his intentions towards her were serious? He'd been highly sought after in Society, and had never shown any interest in anything more than flirtations. Miss Lambert did not seem inclined to accept her cousin either, and who could blame her after his trying to compromise her!

She walked back towards the house pondering the situation. Miss Lambert needed a good marriage, and Dr Craig needed a good wife, especially after his heartbreak with Beatrice. Elly would make sure they had plenty of opportunity to spend time together, and let Nature take its course.

Elly entered the breakfast room and found the Dowager eating alone. "Good morning, Grandmamma." She bent over to kiss the Dowager on the cheek. "I've been walking with Miss Lambert. She is delightful."

"Indeed she is."

"It is a pity she was left in such circumstances."

"I intend to see them changed. What have you done with her?" She torqued her head to look behind Elly.

"I left her with Dr Craig. They were getting along famously, chatting about diseases and her mother," Elly remarked as she walked over towards the sideboard and began filling her plate.

"Elly! Why would you do such a thing?"

She stopped abruptly and turned to look at her grandmother. "Why would I not? He won't try to compromise her, I assure you!"

"Are you losing your sight?"

"Not that I know of." She wrinkled her forehead and turned back to her plate.

"He is charming and handsome," the Dowager said with a hint of exasperation.

"Precisely. They would be an excellent match." Elly took a seat and began to eat.

"Are you so inconstant to your poor brother?"

"I will not countenance that remark, Grandmamma. I have heard that nothing more than a mere friendship exists between Andrew and Miss Lambert. I am thinking of her future."

"Had you seen the two of them together, you would not question his sincerity."

"Then why did he leave to spend an indeterminate amount of time on another continent when she was in a desperate situation?" She took a sip of coffee. "No, I cannot believe Andrew would behave so, were he to be in love with someone."

"I encouraged him to go. Besides, he had promised your father."

"Papa would not have held him to it, had he known."

"Had I known what, dear?" Sir Charles asked as he entered the room and heard his name.

"Grandmamma believes Andrew to be smitten with Miss Lambert."

"Oh, yes, I quite agree," he said in his usual jovial manner.

"Then why ever did you encourage him to leave her?"

"I had intended to establish her in Society to make their way easier," the Dowager said, as if her reasoning should be obvious.

"Andrew doesn't give a fig for Society. Miss Lambert does not seem the type," Elly argued.

"No, that is certainly true, and I cannot blame her after the way her family was shunned. However, I gather she does not feel herself to be worthy of a gentleman such as Andrew. I thought if I could make her see that she belongs there, it would smooth the path for Andrew when he returns."

"I think that is a grave mistake, Grandmamma. I can attempt to keep her from spending excessive time with Dr Craig, but I am afraid that separating them will only serve to convince her that she does not belong with him—that she needs to make her own way. And, if you put her in the pathway of Lord Kendall, who knows what he might try as he becomes more desperate."

"I am inclined to agree with Elly, Henrietta."

The Dowager looked concerned. "It is already done. I own I thought Andrew's trip would be considerably shorter. We will simply have to make certain she does not make her own path. I am capable of putting obstacles in the way of her leaving. She should be safe from Lord Kendall here, at least."

"Then you best pray she is not susceptible to the good doctor's charms," Sir Charles added.

The Dowager cast him a look of reproach.

Elly snorted. "How long do you expect Andrew to be away, Papa?"

"At least until spring, I'm afraid."

"Then we must send Miss Lambert to Andrew."

"I'll not have her crossing the ocean and throwing herself at him. Even if he is my grandson, a lady cannot do such a thing," the Dowager protested.

"What if she were properly chaperoned?" Sir Charles suggested.

"Andrew's neighbours have four unmarried daughters. They are quite rich and fetching. If they do not open their mouths. Who knows what schemes they may come up with to entrap Andrew, should he remain in America long?" Elly taunted. She could see her Grandmamma's mind churning. She cast a look at Sir Charles.

"I admit I would rather not have one of them for my daughter," he opined.

"Who would chaperone?" the Dowager asked.

"I will, of course." Elly stated.

"Easton will never agree to it, and you cannot expect to take the triplets on such a voyage at this age in your condition," Sir Charles reasoned.

"I will ask Nathaniel and Lydia, if I cannot convince Adam," Elly conceded. "I do not think Miss Lambert will agree to this scheme unless she believes she is to take a position."

"Then let her think she is going to help," Sir Charles suggested.

"What if they decided to stay in America? I promised Millicent I would look after her." the Dowager was still sceptical.

"This is looking after her," Elly reasoned.

"We are taking a big gamble. What if we are wrong?"

"I'm gambling on my brother doing right."

"You are gambling on him thinking with his mind," the Dowager muttered.

Chapter Thirteen

Lady Easton hoped her plan of throwing Miss Lambert and Dr Craig together had not already backfired. She found them walking along the path to the cliffs discussing Gwen's mother's illness with passion and animation. She had best discourage furthering this acquaintance quickly.

"How was the seminar?" she asked as she reached the pair.

"Very interesting. Much of it was beyond my understanding, but I do believe it was what my mother suffered from," Gwen remarked.

"I confess I am eager to learn anything I can from you," Dr Craig added.

"I beg your pardon. Am I interrupting?" Elly asked.

"Not at all. I need to check on some of the men. Thank you for sharing your mother's story with me, Miss Lambert," Dr Craig said earnestly.

"Of course. I am happy to oblige anytime you like."

That was what Elly was afraid of. Dr Craig walked back into the school.

"Miss Lambert, would you walk with me?"

"Certainly," she said agreeably.

"Do you mind my speaking frankly?"

"No, of course not."

"Some do, you know. I can never abide those that will not say what they mean."

"I do recall that from my Society days, but those were few and very long ago."

"Yes, my Grandmamma has told me some of your situation. I also

146

heard you and my brother were acquainted."

Gwendolyn blushed, despite wishing she could control it. "Yes, I have had the privilege of becoming friends with Mr Abbott."

"Are you as taken with him as he is with you?"

Gwendolyn was speechless. Had Mr Abbott spoken to his family about her? "I have no notion of his feelings."

"I can see I was too frank, but most ladies in your circumstances would have leapt at your cousin's marriage proposal. My Grandmamma was my informant, as I can see you are wondering. My brother has not broken any confidences. Tell me, Miss Lambert, do you want to go to America? My father said you expressed a desire to travel and went as far as to offer yourself as housekeeper."

"I am not certain what I want to do right now. Or what I would do when I arrived there, but I do want to see the world."

"River's Bend is a heavenly place. I spent six years there, you know. It would be a wonderful opportunity for you. However, going alone would not be quite the thing. Society there is more forgiving, but they still observe certain proprieties. Not that I was ever good at minding them, but I did have my father there to look out for me."

"Your brother has told me some of what it is like. I am certain you are correct, and that it would be difficult for me to establish myself with no connections or money. It was the reason I suggested myself as housekeeper."

"I assumed as much, but it still would not be proper to go alone, you know."

"I had already dismissed showing up at the door as a wanton."

Lady Easton gurgled appreciation. "Perhaps. Perhaps not." Gwen could see the wheels turning in Lady Easton's head. "Has my brother offered you marriage, Miss Lambert?"

Again, Gwendolyn found herself blushing and speechless. "He asked me to go with him."

"I knew it! Miss Lambert…may I call you Gwen? It seems silly to be so formal when we will be sisters."

"I…I…" Gwen struggled to find the proper words.

"My brother would not offer you something improper—gently bred female or no. He often says things without realising how they sound." Elly laughed. "You are not convinced. You do have feelings for him, do you not?"

"You are very frank, Lady Easton." Gwen laughed hesitantly.

"Elly," she corrected. "Yes, but it saves so much time doesn't it? Come. I'd best head back to the house before my husband sends the servants to carry me. I will help you get to America and to Andrew, if that is what you truly wish. There is a boat leaving soon with some men to help Andrew. Leave my Grandmamma to me."

She took Gwen's arm and began to lead her. "And please don't mention service to her again. *Please.*"

"Very well." Gwen changed the subject, overwhelmed by Elly's bluntness. "Are you not ill? I had understood you to be having difficulties."

"Me? Oh, no. I'm in perfect health. My sister is the one with difficulties, and I am a convenient excuse." Elly rubbed on her round belly. "One is not permitted to speak of such things, but her marriage is difficult. She is happier here."

Gwen thought it must be horrible at home for Lady Abernathy if they thought she looked happy here.

"Are you fond of children, Gwen?"

"I have no aversion to them. I've never been around any."

Elly laughed. "Well, now is as good as time as any. We've got a nursery full. Come along and I'll introduce you."

~*~

"Mama! Mama!" little voices cried excitedly when they caught sight of their mother.

Three cherubic toddlers with brilliant blue eyes started running towards Elly and Gwen as they walked towards the house. Elly was summarily squeezed into a hug by all three little people. Instead of chastising, the nurse looked upon the chaos with affection, while Elly laughed. Gwen watched the scene with wonder.

"Children, there is someone I want you to meet. This is our cousin, Miss Lambert. Miss Lambert, this is Garreth, Charles, and Elizabeth."

The three children lined up, a stark contrast to the few moments prior. The two boys made adorable bows and the little girl performed a credible curtsy.

A chorus of "Pweased to meet you," followed.

Gwen returned the curtsy and said hello.

The little boy closest to Elly reached out and tugged slightly on his mother's hand, but remained quiet until she addressed him.

"Yes, Charlie?"

"Gwandpa said we can have a picnic!"

"Picnic? When?"

"Today, Mama!"

The moment of decorum was lost, and all three children felt compelled to join in the excitement of telling her the news.

"We going to fish, Mama!" one insisted.

"No, we going to ride ponies!" another protested.

"No, we going to eat!" the last argued.

"Children! I am certain all of your wishes may be accommodated. But who is seeing to the food?"

"Cook, of cowse."

"And everyone is invited?" She was certain this could not be the case or she would have heard about it.

"Yes."

The boys took Elly's hands, and little Lizzy boldly took Gwen's, and began leading them towards the area by the river designated for such occasions.

Apparently the children had not been mistaken, for there was already a gathering of tables, food and a crowd of people.

Gwen looked to Elly. "You knew nothing of this?"

"Not a thing."

When they reached the table they were able to see a large cake and a buffet of food laid out.

"Happy birthday, Mama!" the children shouted, clearly pleased with themselves for keeping the surprise.

Lord Easton congratulated them and kissed his wife on the cheek.

"Adam, you know I do not like to have a fuss made."

"This was all their doing. I was outnumbered, I'm afraid."

People from the village and many of the orphans and veterans had come out to celebrate. Gwen drifted away from the crowd and watched, still a bit overwhelmed by her present situation.

"You will grow used to it," a Scottish brogue pronounced.

Gwen looked up to see Dr Craig standing before her smiling.

She smiled back. "I suppose. It is much different than my quiet existence in Bath has been. It was only me and my mother for several years."

"I dinna think to offer my condolences earlier. I humbly beg your pardon, and I am verra sorry for your loss."

"Oh, no sir, you did. But thank you, Dr Craig. "

"I'm certain they would understand if you need some quiet. They do realise they are overwhelming to most people." He chuckled.

She had no appropriate response to that, but she smiled.

"Will you be staying on here, then?" he asked.

"I am uncertain. I must find a position, but the Dowager insists I take time for mourning."

"Verra wise of her. You have the rest of your life to find a situation. You need not hurry from here as I'm sure you can see everyone is welcome. I've been tempted to make this my home myself."

"Where do you live? I am certain Lady Easton told me, but I've forgotten."

"My accent must be failing me. I live in Scotland. I make occasional visits here to the school to teach."

She tried not to wince at her stupidity. "I've never been to Scotland. I hear it is beautiful."

"Aye. There is no place like it."

"I believe some of my father's family hails from there."

He glanced at her hair and simply said, "I doona doubt it."

Her cheeks pinked becomingly, and he continued, "You would be verra welcome there any time. There is also an orphanage run by Lord and Lady Vernon, who is also Lord Fairmont's sister. I'm certain if you doona find a position here, you would find one there."

"Gwen! Gwen!"

She turned to see the octogenarian Dowager scrambling hurriedly towards her.

"Ma'am? Are you unwell?" Gwen went to her. She had never seen the regal lady lacking composure before.

"I'm fine, but Elly needs your help."

"My help? Is the baby coming? Perhaps Dr Craig..."

"No, no nothing of the sort." She waved her hand dismissively. "Hurry along now."

"Very well. Thank you, Dr Craig. I will keep in mind what you said."

He tipped his hat and she walked off with the Dowager, who was dragging her precipitously towards Elly.

"Here is Gwen." The Dowager presented her to Elly.

"Hello, Gwen." Elly said looking at her grandmother mysteriously. "We have met, Grandmamma."

"Yes, you needed her help remember?"

"I did?" Gwen saw the Dowager nudge Elly. "Of course I did!"

"Famous!" the Dowager exclaimed. "I will be off now then."

The two ladies watched the Dowager walk away quickly.

"You do not need me, do you?"

"Not particularly, but I am always happy to see you. It would be a shame if Grandmamma was losing her wits, but I suppose it happens to the best of us at some point."

Elly glanced over Gwen's shoulder and saw her grandmother making hand motions towards Dr Craig. She gave a swift nod of understanding, and drew Gwen away towards the children who were shouting.

"Mama! Lizzy put worms down my shirt again," Charlie said indignantly.

"Coming, dears!" The expectant mother hurried after her little tomboy.

~*~

Gwen arrived back at her room from the picnic, her head spinning. It was as if Elly already had her and Andrew married in her mind. She could not allow herself to dream of such a thing. She could see herself keeping house; she had done that since her mother became ill. What did she have to lose by going, she wondered? If she hated America, she could always leave. She would not be any worse off than she was before. Well, before she arrived here.

Mr Abbott would not be remaining in America. She might not even see him by the time she arrived. She wanted to make sure her motives in going there were pure. She could not deny that she longed to see him again, however. She felt a twinge of anticipation at a chance to see a new place.

There was a knock on her door.

"Enter."

"Good day, Miss. I am Josie. I am Lady Easton's maid, of sorts. She sent these dresses for you, seeing as she doesn't need them right now."

Josie was followed in by several servants carrying a variety of dark gowns.

Gwen opened her mouth to protest.

"It twon't do no good, miss. You might as well accept. These Abbott ladies are a force of nature," Josie laughed.

"I can see that," Gwen said as she looked about her in astonishment.

"It is just their way of showing affection. If you don't accept these, they will send for the dressmaker. Lady Easton thought you would prefer this."

Gwen nodded slightly.

"If you feel guilty about accepting their charity, you should go and peek at the orphanage school and the home for wounded soldiers.

They've made it their life's work to help people. Besides, you're family. If they've taken in all manner of strangers, why wouldn't they want you, too?"

Gwen simply could not wrap her mind around the situation she found herself in.

"You'll grow accustomed to it. I was taken in by Sir Charles and Lady Easton near ten years ago in America. They truly are as wonderful as they seem."

"Did you like it—America?"

"'Twere my home, miss. I still miss it, but I've got a husband 'ere and, of course, Miss Elly."

"Would you go back?"

"In a heartbeat. But I'm happy here, too."

A footman knocked with his hands full of art supplies.

"Set 'm over there," Josie directed the boy.

"I'll leave you to it, then. I've got lessons to help with at the school. You should come visit again one day."

"Thank you, I would like that very much."

~*~

Miss Lambert,

May I offer my deepest condolence. I wish I could have offered you my personal support. Gran says you refuse to accept her generosity and are insistent upon going into service! What madness is this? Please do not accept a position at present. Take time to grieve before throwing yourself at the mercy of an unknowing patron. I assure you, you will be of no bother to my grandmother, if you can tolerate her whims. She means well. I cannot bear to think of you slaving as a governess or maid to some slovenly or un-slovenly master or mistress. I had hoped to be returned by now, for the autumn is arriving and I do not wish for a winter crossing. Rebuilding is quite a daunting task. Abe has maintained the fields but had to neglect the house to do so. He was unable to find a steward willing to work with or be hired by a man of colour. Ignorance abounds everywhere, however. I cannot say it is a problem solely endemic to America. Dare I hope you will still be under the protection of my family upon my return? Please do not allow them to frighten you away.

With affection,
Andrew Abbott

~*~

Mr Abbott,

You will be pleased to know I am currently with your grandmother in Sussex at the Dower House. She refuses to help me find a position until I have passed the initial stage of mourning. She is most gracious, as is all of your family. It is quite an operation they have established here for the orphans and veterans. Perhaps I may consider teaching here if they will have me. I know nothing of medicine, and little of horses, so I am not certain how I may help. I dare not broach the topic with the Dowager yet.

I am engaged in painting a picture for your sister and Lord Easton. It is my first attempt at the real sea. I hope I may provide a worthy copy for them. Does the rebuilding progress? Have you found a steward yet?
Your friend,
Gwendolyn Lambert

When Gwen was painting, she lost herself. Her troubles and sorrows faded away, and there was nothing but her and her vision. It was similar to the escape she found in books, though she was able to create her own version of a happy ending. Today, as she captured a perfect sunrise, one that she had waited nearly a week for, she dreamt of sailing off into the horizon and into Mr Abbott's waiting arms. But she should not allow herself to even dream!

She had sent a refusal letter to her cousin. Most would think her stupid and ungrateful to turn down such an offer, but she had thought, slept and prayed about the situation and could not feel comfortable. She had been miserable at Kendall House, and had decided she would rather earn her bread than be Peregrine's viscountess. She could not marry a man she could not respect, even if it meant going into service instead.

She was still toying with the idea of going to America. Everything seemed perfect, but it all depended on Andrew's reaction to her arrival. Could she be content alone in America if she were to arrive and find him gone? She paused to contemplate that.

She would not have a choice. She would be forced to stay there until she could afford to return.

The more she thought on it, the real question was, would she be content to stay in England? The trip would fulfill her dream to travel to worlds unknown. She thought life would be better with Mr Abbott, but she would not regret it, if only because she had always wanted to see the world.

She inhaled a deep breath of sea air, and felt the mist from the spray of a rogue wave. This was lovely. The Eastons, Fairmonts and Abbotts had been incredibly welcoming and generous. She knew how fortunate she was. She would be scrubbing floors or standing on a street corner earning her keep were it not for their charity. She should be content here. But she still felt alone, incomplete, as if there was something or someone missing.

A voice inside her screamed to take the chance. To go after him, to take the adventure in the new land. She thought of everything Elly had told her about her brother. *He would not have offered something improper. He was smitten with her.* It was hard for her to believe, but had he not been constant in his letters? She did not want to wait and let a harpy compromise him or convince him to marry them.

The thought of that was enough to send her pulse racing. She put the finishing touches on the canvas and hurried back to the house to let Elly know she would go to America. She decided to carry the painting herself and send a footman back for the easel.

As she walked, encumbered by the large canvas she was attempting to keep from smudging, she felt a sense of relief at having made a decision. She was reassured by the family's confidence in Mr Abbott, and comforted herself with the knowledge that she had a plan in place, should she have misunderstood his intentions. She hoped River's Bend was as glorious as Sussex. She had enjoyed her time here, but felt almost giddy at the chance to see the world—and Mr Abbott again.

"What has put the smile on your face, Cousin? Because I do not feel like smiling."

Gwen jumped, and almost lost her balance and the painting. "Peregrine!"

"Surprised to see me, Cuz?" he said sarcastically.

"Actually, yes. Did you receive my letter?"

"That is why I have come."

"I do not understand."

"I hope to still change your mind."

"I am sorry, Cousin Peregrine, but I cannot marry you."

"If you find me so repulsive, you may live elsewhere. I have no objection, once you provide me with an heir."

Gwen felt her skin begin to crawl and had to hold back a shudder.

"I am sorry." She shook her head.

"Is there someone else?"

She looked away.

"Who is it? What can he offer you that I cannot?"

"I do not have to answer that."

He grabbed her wrist. "I am sorry to have to do this, Cousin, but you will thank me later."

"No!" She shouted. "Let me go!"

He began to pull her down the path, and she tried to wrest her arm from him while holding on to the painting.

"Drop the blasted painting!" he said, irritated.

"Unhand her, Kendall!" a deep voice boomed, as the sound of a pistol cocked.

Peregrine froze. "Fairmont, there has been a misunderstanding."

"I agree. The lady said she would not marry you and wishes to be let go. I am uncertain how that could be misunderstood. Easton, did you hear her say something else?"

Easton showed himself with his pistol cocked and pointed at Lord Kendall. "No, I heard the same thing quite clearly."

"I thought so. Miss Lambert, if you are comfortable walking back to the house, Easton and I would like to have a word with Lord Kendall."

"Of course."

"My painting was not harmed, was it, Miss Lambert?" Easton asked tritely while Nathaniel kept the gun pointed at Lord Kendall.

"I do not believe so."

Easton took a look and was satisfied. "Lovely. Thank you."

She hurried on to the house and hoped they resolved her cousin's misunderstandings with fisticuffs rather than pistols. For all he had been grossly out of line, she did not wish his blood on her hands.

"What happened?" Elly was waiting for her at the door. She signalled for Hendricks to take the painting.

"I do not even know. I was painting and I was happy, and I decided to go to America, and then he was there." She managed to string a few coherent words together.

"Who? I saw a carriage drive up. I sent Adam out to investigate when it didn't stop at the house. We are wary of strangers with the children and veterans."

"Lord Kendall."

She saw Elly's face tighten.

"But Lord Fairmont and Easton were there. I don't know what would have happened if they hadn't intervened." Gwen had no idea how she was able to speak calmly. Her insides were churning, and she was subconsciously rubbing her wrists where Peregrine had pulled her.

"You poor dear. This is getting out of hand. Something is going to have to be done."

"I believe he is being taught a lesson at the moment."

"Most assuredly, if I know Adam and Nathaniel, but they won't kill him. He might try again."

"Do you think he would dare?"

"He obviously thinks you are the one he needs to wed. So unless you are married or gone, I don't think he will give up." She paused. "That's it!"

"Pardon?"

"You said you decided you would go to America!"

"I did."

"Then you will be leaving sooner than you planned."

Chapter Fourteen

What had she done? Feelings of uncertainty and self-doubt washed over her and she struggled to breath. Gwen felt the boat list beneath her as she looked around her tiny cabin that had no windows, and tried to reassure herself the walls were not in reality closing in on her. Her stomach churned and beads of perspiration gathered on her brow. Suddenly, the rashness of her hasty decision hit her with a hefty dose of regret. She wished herself back home in Bath with her mother. Tears streamed down her cheeks as she thought about what had brought her to this moment. If only she could be reassured she was making the right choice.

She musn't dwell on what she could not change. She decided some fresh air would remedy her doldrums, but when she stood she felt green. She empathised with Mr Abbott's sea malady, and wondered how she would survive weeks of this.

Gwen was not alone on her journey, however. It was humourous how many chaperones she had. Five of the veterans have volunteered to go to America. Buffy and Josie were to take on the stewardship duties, and Lord and Lady Fairmont decided to visit and help out for a time. They had never been to America and thought they would enjoy the holiday. Gwen was certain they were too polite to say otherwise.

As Gwen was feeling green, she was not sure it was worth it after all. She secretly thought that Lady Fairmont's presence was the only reason the Dowager had agreed to let her go. If it did not work out, she would have a means of transport back to England, and would have been respectably chaperoned the entire time. Gwen had not been able to make the Dowager understand that it did not matter. There was little hope for her being respectable in the Beau Monde. The Dowager had protested, but she had consented. Especially when Elly insisted the scheming Bradley girls were likely sinking their claws into Andrew as they spoke, and that Lord Kendall would continue his pursuit until he succeeded.

Elly had put up a fight about going with them. She desperately wanted to go back to her beloved plantation. But Lord Easton would hear nothing of it as she was in a delicate situation.

Hence, there they were on a private schooner hired by the family to transport a small army of them to America. As nausea was overtaking her normally robust constitution, Gwen prayed Lord Fairmont was correct; she would grow accustomed to the sea and would not be ill the entire way, or she might not be able to leave America once she arrived.

After depositing her snack in her chamber pot, she decided to venture up to the deck to see if fresh air and sunshine would orient her and alleviate her sea sickness.

She refused to be sick for their month-long trip across the sea; she needed to find something with which to occupy her time. Elly had made sure she had ample sketching and painting supplies, but she had no idea what Elly thought she would find to draw on this ship for weeks as she looked around and saw nothing but water and boat.

She gazed at the powerful sails and the masts that reached towards the sky. She contemplated and decided it would make an interesting picture.

"As I have little else to do," she muttered to herself, "it will not hurt to try." She opened her sketch pad and found a place to sit and work. She reflected as she worked, and wondered if she could forge a living through her art. Mr Scott had sold her painting for fifty pounds, and the Eastons had paid her one hundred pounds for the scene she had painted for them! Likely it had been a charity offering for mediocre work, but they had insisted they could not be more delighted and commissioned her to paint River's Bend. At least she would not be obliged to hurry into a position out of destitution if she disliked it there.

She became absorbed in trying to capture the wind's effect on the sails.

"Why are you drawing a picture of the sails, miss?" a young voice asked.

Without looking up she answered, "I've never drawn them before."

"Is it difficult? My drawings look nothing like yours." The little girl moved in closer and looked over Gwen's shoulder.

"I don't suppose they are too difficult. If you know basic drawing techniques."

Amelia sighed. "I've been trying to learn, but my art master thinks I'm a hopeless case."

"You've taken lessons then?" Gwen looked up to the blue-eyed beauty who was a miniature replica of her father, Lord Fairmont.

Amelia nodded. "How did you make the sails look real?"

"By using dimensions. I used some shadow here and here." Gwen demonstrated the technique. "Would you like to try?"

The little girl looked hesitant but nodded. She drew a line behind one of the sails and then studied it.

"Keep going," Gwen encouraged.

Amelia repeated her lines until they were similar to the ones Gwen had made.

"Excellent. Now take your finger and blend the lines just so." Gwen demonstrated effortlessly.

"Brilliant! Miss Lambert, will you be my new art mistress? I must show Papa!" The little girl grabbed the sketchpad and ran off. Gwen watched after her longingly, remembering a time when she had been as excited about art and her life. She smiled. At least she knew now how she could pass her journey.

~*~

Twenty-one days down and no end in sight. Gwen was certain she had grown fins and scales with all the sea foods she'd been obliged to eat. She also could not remember the last time she had been bored. She had been too sick to consider it overly much, but today the seas were calm and she was able to think about something other than where the nearest basin was. She was not sure how she had maintained sanity before she'd had chores. There was nothing for her to do to help out. The ship was fully staffed, and there were too many men about for her to wander. She was supposed to be attended by another female if she wanted to leave her cabin; she'd been informed of that after venturing out alone the first day. Josie, Amelia and Lady Fairmont were the only other females aboard, so her choices were limited.

She was debating how to spend her idle time before the Fairmonts rose for the day. She eyed the stack of books Lady Easton had sent with her and she looked towards her sketch pad. She decided against drawing. She might need to amuse Lady Amelia along the way, and did not want to be frivolous with the pages should they be on the sea longer than anticipated, heaven forbid.

The stack of books called to her. Some of her favourites were also loved by Lady Easton, and she had lent her copies for the trip. She looked at the two books that Mr Abbott had given her. She laughed. She definitely did not want to read *Robinson Crusoe* while aboard a ship. She doubted she would last one month alone on an island, let alone eight and twenty years! Thankfully, she had read that before she set sail. She picked up *Gulliver's Travels* and decided to give it a try. She had heard of the book, of course, but had never particularly been interested in reading it before Mr Abbott gave it to her.

The book began with another shipwreck. What had Mr Abbott been thinking of by having her read these? He had not been thinking of her boarding a ship to venture to America.

She was keen to like *Gulliver's Travels* at Mr Abbott's recommendation, and while she appreciated the satire, she had never been much for politics unless it involved human rights or equality for all people. That was one way in which she was uncertain of the new American government; it proclaimed equality, yet allowed slavery.

Gwen continued on through the pages. She got through Gulliver's treason and escaping Lilliput, and was saved by a knock on the door.

"Enter," she bade her guest.

"Miss Lambert?"

"Come in, Amelia." She looked up from the book to smile at her new friend.

"Mama sent me to see if you care to take breakfast with us, or if we can have something brought to you?"

"Yes, I would love to breakfast with you, thank you."

"What were you reading?" she asked curiously.

"*Gulliver's Travels.*"

"I love *Gulliver's Travels!*" Amelia exclaimed.

"You do?" Gwen said with disbelief.

"Yes, I think it would be famous to be a giant or to live amongst them. As long as I was in favour, of course."

"Of course. Only, I had not thought it a book for children."

"Mama lets me read most everything. She says she was raised by books."

Gwen was amused by the young lady's understanding, and thought perhaps she might enjoy the story more if she observed it from a child's perspective as a fantastic fairytale, rather than reading into the underlying messages. The two entered the next cabin where breakfast was laid out. Lady Fairmont and her son were sitting at the small table in the captain's cabin which had been purloined for use by the Fairmonts. It was much larger than her own cabin, and had windows that allowed in light and a view of the sea. Gwen thought that she might not feel so ill if she had a window, for when she could see, it helped immensely. She would never say such a thing, for the Fairmonts would feel obliged to give her their cabin, or allow her to sleep there in Lord Fairmont's place.

"You look much less green today, Miss Lambert. Are you feeling better?" Lady Fairmont greeted her.

"I am, thank you. I believe the seas are much calmer."

"Yes. That certainly helps. Amelia was hoping you would be able to play cards with us today. With Josie, that makes for four of us."

"That would be a welcome diversion. It has been years since I have played cards."

"I am certain you will pick it up again. I must have something to do to keep my mind from dwelling on how much longer we will be at sea. I would make a dreadful Navy man."

"Fortunately for you, Mama, they do not allow women in the Navy."

"I suppose so, dear."

Gwen looked at Robert, the Fairmonts' son. He was very intent on eating his breakfast. When he finished, he immediately climbed down from the table and went straight for his toy soldiers.

"Bang! Bang! Dead frog!" He mimicked two soldiers fighting.

Gwen had to suppress her laughter.

"Robert William, please try to be less violent, dear. Are all boys born wanting to shoot guns and arrows?" Lady Fairmont looked to Gwen, incredulous.

"My brother certainly seemed that way," Gwen remarked.

"Mama, it is because he plays with the soldiers at home," Amelia said matter-of-factly.

"I suppose so. I will never free the sounds of Waterloo from my mind."

"You were there?" Gwen asked in astonishment.

"Yes. That is where Lord Fairmont received his injuries."

"We thought Papa was dead for a long time," Amelia explained to Gwen.

"I cannot imagine not knowing," Gwen said reverently, though she had lost her brother.

"I hope you never have to," Lady Fairmont replied quietly.

Josie looked around the door. "Is it time for cards?"

"Please come in."

"We were telling Gwen we needed a fourth player."

"I'm quite out of practice." Gwen was wary of cards, for they had been her father's downfall. Surely they would not be playing for stakes with a child among them?

"How are the men faring up on deck, Josie?" Lady Fairmont asked.

"Oh, I think they all fancy themselves sailors. Talking shop about winds and knots and all other sorts of foreign language. Get aft of the boat or afore the mast. Sleep in a berth and belay the rope..." She shook her head in dismay.

"They create their own talk to feel important," Amelia said astutely as she shuffled the cards. The child did not seem to be a mere nine years the way she spoke.

"I 'spect you're right, dear. I only wanted to know if the winds were favourable. I wasn't asking for equations about arcs, angles and acceleration."

All the ladies laughed.

"I'm certainly happy to have company I understand," Gwen remarked.

"Amen," Josie agreed.

"Miss Josie, what will America be like?" Amelia asked.

"Hm. Well, the weather is warmer most of the time, though it snows once or twice a winter. It's very big, and the place we are going is only a very small part of the country. This time of year is warm and has beautiful sunsets. But mostly, it is not very different from England."

"It isn't?"

"Mind you, I've only been in the one place, but the people are much the same. There isn't as much fancy society, but people here work hard and people there work hard. In fact, many of the folk you will see came from England."

"What is River's Bend like?"

Josie's face took on a dreamy look as she told of the manor house on the river, and the vast fields of crops and vineyards that were grown there.

"It sounds very romantic," Amelia said wistfully.

"Is there anything else near?" Lydia asked practically.

"Oh, certainly. You can reach Alexandria or Washington travelling a few miles in either direction."

Hearing Josie speak about River's Bend made Gwen think that it must indeed be a magical place. Josie spoke of all the fun and adventure she and Elly had had there together. She had also heard Elly tell stories and about how she missed her old home as they had prepared to leave. She could not help but daydream about what life would be like there in case she never returned to England.

She tried to dampen her anticipation and expectation of Mr Abbott's reception of her, but it was very difficult not to include him on her grand adventure. She often replayed their brief week together over and over in her mind. But for some, it was out of sight out of mind. It had been several months since that fateful day when he'd left, and even though he wrote to her, it might only have been out of pity. He had been most attentive—she was certain she was not wrong. What she was not certain of was the manner of proposal he intended, being so beneath his touch as she was. It was ridiculous to think he could have meant marriage.

Elly had assured Gwen that the Dowager had said he was enamoured when she'd had second thoughts about boarding the ship. He would not have invited her to join him were his love not assured. Those were heady statements indeed. However, she tried to maintain some measure of rational thought. Perhaps his family did not know him as well as they thought, she supposed. It was not uncommon in Society for a gentleman to keep a mistress. Marriages were arrangements of wealth, property and bloodlines in the aristocracy, which made her a highly undesirable candidate for wife. A ladybird was all gentlemen had thought her fit for after her father's downfall, and she would never forget the shame she felt when those gentleman had made their intentions known. She knew deep down her worth should not be measured by Society's standards, but it was hard to overcome that experience. She could not stop herself from dreaming when alone with her thoughts, but she scarce dared to hope her destiny could be that of becoming Mrs Abbott.

As the days passed on the seemingly endless sea, she tried to focus on the peace and serenity. If she stayed in her cabin she began to feel her sanity escaping her. Her grief was raw and her future uncertain, and it became easy to doubt. It was a small measure of comfort to feel the wind in her face and sail into the horizon, and believe that her mother was watching over her journey.

Nearly one hundred drawings, twenty books and thousands of card games later, someone shouted 'land ho!' Never before had Gwen properly appreciated earth, grass and trees. Some things one had to do without in order to appropriately miss them.

~*~

Andrew had found some workers to help rebuild the house, but they were not moving quickly enough for his liking. They worked diligently while he was around, but he had no notion if they would do so were he to leave. He had acquired many skills in this venture, not to mention calloused hands and sore muscles.

As he watched the summer fade into autumn, he was afraid he would be away from Miss Lambert until the spring. From the sound of his grandmother's letters, he did not think she would wait for him. He had been parted from her several months already. But he would find her, no matter, and hope it wasn't too late. Absence was perhaps making his heart grow fonder—if that were possible—and he did not want to imagine life without her.

He helped nearly every day, but rebuilding was still a slow process. They had managed to enclose the house and paint it, therefore it looked whole from the outside at least, leaving only ten more rooms until freedom. His father had written of sending a steward from England, and he watched hopefully every day for his arrival, but thus far the only visitors had been ladies throwing their eligible daughters in his path.

Even their belief that he had an intended did not deter them much.

He enjoyed the tasty baskets of baked goods and home brew they offered, but he could not find temptation in any of them personally. If Miss Lambert would not have him, he would not have anyone. She owned his heart. He sat on the porch swing he had built for relaxation after a hard day's work and kicked up his feet. He had just taken a sip of lemonade when he heard carriage wheels. He muttered curses under his breath and decided against putting his sweaty shirt back on. Who could it be at this hour? He wasn't in any condition for unannounced visitors.

He began laughing at the sight the visitors would be presented with, and the gentleman in him won out.

"It would serve them right."

Everyone about knew the plantation was being rebuilt and he wasn't entertaining. This was not the time of day that people visited without an invitation. He sat back down and drank his lemonade hastily. He was not going to waste his hard earned treat. He continued with his feet up, hoping the carriage would realise it had taken a wrong turn.

The plantation workers had all settled in for the night in their cottages. Everyone worked hard and therefore turned in early, Andrew included. He would be more lonely were he not so exhausted from labour. But every evening before turning in he would sit here on the porch and dream of his green-eyed, flame-haired goddess and what it would be like to kiss her.

"I should have kissed her before I left," he muttered to himself. He had never regretted anything more. Perhaps she would not have doubted me, he thought smugly. Or perhaps she would have doubted my intentions were honourable. He shook his head and tossed a nearby pebble as the carriage grew closer.

He eyed his rancid shirt with distaste and decided to walk himself and his shirt over to the water for a quick rinse. He had taken to bathing in the river. Why would he bathe indoors when he had Nature's bathtub at his doorstep? He grabbed the bar of soap he kept on the ledge and took a refreshing plunge. He had some new plumbing inventions installed in the house to include indoor water closets and faucets, but he had not yet tried the bathing apparatus. He rather liked bathing at sunset.

The sounds of the carriage came closer. He was trying to determine who the visitors were before committing himself, but it was growing too dark to make anything out. He had best come out of the water to see. There was boat traffic this evening, and they wouldn't be able to see him in the dark anyway.

A boat came nearer and nearer to his landing, and carriages still sounded in the distance. Was the long-awaited steward here at last? He ran into the house and changed into some dry clothes and was walking back towards the landing with a lantern when he spied a rather large party of men landing.

"Ahoy there!" one of them yelled.

"Welcome!" Andrew yelled excitedly and waved his arms as if he was Crusoe being rescued. "Who goes there?"

"Major Abbott?" He heard a familiar voice.

"Buffy?" Would it be highly inappropriate if he gave him a hug? He was so relieved to see a familiar face. He settled for shaking his arm with vigour.

"Yes, sir. I brought along five men to help us."

"I could kiss your feet, Buffy."

A carriage pulled up near the house, and they all turned to see the arrivals.

"I'm a popular man tonight, Buffy. Unfortunately, it is seldom a welcome visitor."

"That must be Lord Fairmont with the ladies. They were sick of being on a boat."

"The ladies?" He swallowed hard. Dared he hope? His pulse began to race and he was more nervous than he'd been at any time in Wellington's service. He'd had too much time alone to think. What should he do? He always said something acerbic. It was his best mode of defence. But this was Gwen, and she'd just lost everything. For once, humour did not seem suitable.

The carriage opened to reveal Mrs Bradley, followed by her eldest daughter, Jenny. *Oh God above, please help me not to strangle them*, he thought. Suddenly sarcasm did not seem inapt.

"Good evening, Mrs Bradley, Miss Bradley. My company from England has only just arrived. I believe the carriage behind you is carrying the ladies."

"Oh, dearest me. I had not realized you were expecting such a large party," Mrs Bradley said, as she blatantly surveyed the crew of men approaching from the landings as a mother of four unmarried daughters would.

He had only mentioned the imminent arrival of his family every time he had spoken with Mrs Bradley during the past month since he'd learned of it. He desperately wanted to dispose of her and her daughter before his visitors arrived. Instead, Miss Bradley took the opportunity to boldly wind her arm through his and behave as though she were mistress of the manor.

"Aren't you going to introduce me to your guests?" Jenny suggested.

"I apologise, ladies, but it is growing late and I am certain the arrivals will wish to be settled and rest. Perhaps we may meet for a proper introduction soon," he said cordially, but with finality. He walked them towards their carriage and tried to usher them in. Mrs Bradley was speechless for once.

"We shall throw a welcome party for them," she blurted, trying to stall her departure.

"Very considerate of you, ma'am. Good day!" he practically shouted as he shut the door and signalled to the driver.

The other carriage pulled to a stop, and the door opened and Amelia poured out.

"Uncle Andrew!" She ran and barrelled in to his arms. That would never get old.

"Amelia!" Lady Fairmont chastised while laughing.

"She has a few more years to polish her technique. How are you, Lydia?" Andrew said as he opened his arms.

"Very well, Andrew, but most happy to be off the ship." She reached up and kissed him on the cheek.

"Not so happy as Miss Lambert, I'll wager." Lord Fairmont said dryly, as he exited with their son sleeping on his shoulder.

Andrew's breath caught in his throat. She was here. She'd actually come! He had to stop himself from jumping into the carriage and driving off. He longed to welcome her properly. He was thankful he had rid himself of the unwelcome appendage of Miss Bradley on his arm.

"Where is she?" he asked, as he walked to the door of the carriage and peeked his head in. Gwen was sitting in the corner crying. When he saw that, he had no choice but to climb in and wrap his arms around her.

"What's the matter, dearest Gwen? Are those tears of happiness to see me?" he teased.

She hiccoughed a laugh. "Insufferable, odious man! You won't even allow me to cry seriously."

He inhaled the most pleasant scent from her glorious hair. "What should I think when you arrive crying?"

"I thought it would be marvellous to travel abroad. But I should not have come."

"Now, now. Do not be so hasty in your judgement, or I might take it personally. You have not had a proper meal for over a month, I gather."

"It would not matter if I had."

"I assume the sea agrees with you about as well as it agrees with me."

She nodded.

"Let us get you inside. Once you've eaten and had a good night's sleep, everything will seem better in the morning."

He handed her out of the carriage and walked her into the house. Seeing Miss Lambert happy was his primary concern. He fervently hoped that Gwen's tears were not from having caught sight of Miss Bradley and assuming the worst.

Chapter Fifteen

Gwen was relieved to be on dry land, but as she looked around at this strange country, she felt conflicting emotions. The city of Washington had been large and daunting, and looked nothing like Bath, though it paled in comparison to London. She was somewhat relieved to cross the Potomac River and into the countryside. They soon reached the gates of the plantation, and it was an incredible sight as the sun was beginning to set. They rode through fields of tobacco and vineyard-covered hills, before entering a wooded parkland. When the trees stopped, a beautiful white mansion stood before them abutted by a large river. It was unlike anything she had ever seen. Her sketch had not begun to do it justice. She was already itching to begin painting it.

Her eyes drifted towards the crowd of people standing before the house. Her palms began to sweat as she searched nervously for his face. At last she found it, and next to him, arm-in-arm, was a beautiful, elegantly dressed young woman with perfectly coiffed brunette curls. Gwen shrunk into the corner of the carriage with her heart in her throat. She knew she had made a grave mistake. She had not fully thought through what would happen when she arrived, but she had not expected to see another woman on his arm!

Tears fell from her eyes and the magnitude of what she had done hit her with full force. This was not how it was supposed to turn out. No, in storybooks, the heroine did not go chasing after her prince. He was supposed to come to her. Yet here she was throwing herself at his feet. Of course he had found someone else of his own station. She was disgusted with herself and filled with remorse for her naivety. She should never have listened to Andrew's family. Of course they would think him a saint!

Oh, how she wished she could wake up from this horrid nightmare and reverse time! How could she have been so stupidly blind to sanity? She had not considered all of the repercussions. If only she'd had the time to think. How could she have known, living a sheltered life in a small town with no worldly experience? She missed her mother's guidance desperately. Even though the past six years had been a struggle, they were still familiar, and she had been with her mother. She had never felt so alone as she did now. She had no claim to Mr Abbott, no understanding. How could she have allowed herself to become carried away and lost to proper reason?

She was fully dependent on these people for everything. They were not truly family—the connection was minute at best. She had too much pride to be a leech on them, no matter their protests to the contrary.

She would insist on working while she was here and help finish the work at River's Bend, and then she would return with the Fairmonts as soon as possible. She could go back and teach at a school. If not, she would find a way. She had to. But first, she was going to have to figure out how to face Mr Abbott—and the lady in his life.

Suddenly, Mr Abbott had climbed into the carriage and found her crying. His arms were wrapped around her and she felt a flood of mixed emotions. She wanted to melt into his arms, but her acute embarrassment and confusion at the scene she had just witnessed left her stiff. How dared he be so inconsiderate as to hold her moments after touching another woman?

Her first instinct was to run and hide, but he began jesting with her and she found it difficult to think with his arms around her. His nearness made her stupid with discomfort and conflicting emotions.

Before she knew what was happening, she was being ushered out of the carriage, into the house and up the stairs to a bedroom.

Lady Fairmont was hugging her, Josie was searching through her trunks, and brandy-laced tea was thrust before her. Before she knew what had hit her, she was in a nightgown and being tucked into bed with sweet reassurances that she would feel more the thing with a proper night's sleep.

Gwen hated being fussed over, but she was glad to be left alone. She was too full of emotion—mainly anger with herself.

~*~

Andrew was enjoying a cup of coffee in the breakfast room the next morning, when Lord and Lady Fairmont entered looking exhausted.

"Did you not enjoy the crickets singing to you?" Andrew asked sarcastically.

He was given a look that would have melted a lesser man.

"You still do a mean leer, even with one eye. It only wants the quizzing glass for the finishing touch."

"The house looks better than I expected." Nathaniel said, ignoring Andrew.

"And you look very...." Lydia looked him over, noticing his brown skin and rough hands.

"Common? Labourish? Devillish handsome?" Andrew suggested.

"I wasn't going to be quite so tactless," she said with a grin. "It suits you."

He playfully tossed his napkin at her.

"It's not such a bad thing here to work. At least, it hasn't seemed to deter any of them. In fact, the more you work, the more respected you are."

"Are you a choice commodity then?"

"Once you see the available commodities you will understand. Everything is quite spread out here. They do not concentrate their nobility into one city for a marriage mart."

"They do not care for nobility at all, do they? Wasn't that part of the reason for the revolution?" Lord Fairmont reasoned.

"Partly. They may not care for titles and wealth by birthright, but you'll find them quite eager to make their fortune and name."

"I cannot blame them for that."

"Nor can I." They all sipped their coffee, pondering.

"What is left to accomplish?"

"The interior of the guest wing, mainly. I will be glad to have the ladies' help with that."

"Of course. Perhaps one lady more than another?" Lydia prodded.

He sat silent for a moment.

"I have done something stupid."

"And this surprises you?" Nathaniel teased in a brotherly fashion.

He told Lydia and Nathaniel of the town's belief that he was betrothed.

"Why is that such a bad thing? It sounds like you had to protect yourself."

"If only that had worked. The worst part is I told them her name. They would not believe me otherwise."

"You could have made a name up." Nathaniel argued.

"You didn't!" Lydia understood the cause of Andrew's hesitation.

"I did."

"You have to tell her."

"It would seem as though it would be that simple. But her reaction to seeing me did not give me confidence."

179

"She is only tired and still grieving, I'm afraid. She will be better directly. I'm certain she will be delighted to discover she is betrothed."

"Certainly. If only she had not refused me when I asked in England," he stated in his usual tone of sarcasm.

"Pardon?" Lydia asked, stunned. "This makes no sense!"

"I was hoping her refusal was due to her mother's poor health," he said sheepishly.

"But why would she come here if she refused you?" she asked doubtfully.

"Might it have something to do with Lord Kendall trying to force her to marry him?" Nathaniel suggested.

"What has Kendall to do with her?" Andrew demanded.

"They are cousins. The current Lord Kendall's father cut the family off, but the new one claims he wants to protect her and marry her."

"Marry her? Young Kendall the fop?" Andrew was taken aback.

"Yes. Easton thought it smelled wrong and attempted to question the solicitor, but all we knew when we left was Kendall was below the hatches and needed to marry for an inheritance."

"While I understand why he would want to marry Miss Lambert, it doesn't fadge with him."

"True, the Kendalls don't breach good *ton*," Lydia agreed.

"Nevertheless, he attempted to compromise her, then tried the civil route, then tried to abduct her."

"Please tell me he was taught a lesson," Andrew remarked, barely controlling his anger.

"Indeed."

"I envy you that. Have you seen her this morning?"

"No, but I can do so now." Lydia began to rise.

"No, allow me, please."

Lydia raised an eyebrow, but sat back down. "You best tell her."

Nathaniel smiled amusedly into his cup.

Andrew went in search of Miss Lambert. He would tell her and confess his need—no, his love—for her, and convince her to marry him. But she was not in her room. The door was open and the bed made up.

That's odd, Andrew thought. He could not have missed her on the way to the breakfast room. She would not have taken the long route through the wing under construction, for it was cordoned off. He looked about and in the guest chambers and went to the nursery. She was nowhere to be found. He made his way back down to the ground floor, where he encountered Josie.

"Good morning, Josie. Have you seen Miss Lambert?"

"Good morning, sir. Yes, she is in the housekeeper's room speaking with Cook."

"Why ever would she do that?"

"Pardon my saying so, but don't be daft."

"Apparently I am daft, Josie. Would you please explain it to me? In simple terms, mind you."

"She believes she came here to be housekeeper."

That caught him off guard. "I thought that honour was to be yours, Josie."

"You are welcome to argue with her, sir. She insists on earning her keep."

"And she calls me insufferable," Andrew muttered under his breath. "Thank you, Josie. If you want anything, you need only ask. As far as I am concerned, you are the housekeeper. I will deal with Miss Lambert."

She chuckled. "This ought to be amusing. I wish Miss Elly were here to witness this."

~*~

He walked towards the housekeeper's rooms, beginning to fume as he thought on it more. How could she think to work here? She was going to marry him and they were to live happily ever after on the country estate in Hampshire, or wherever her heart fancied—an Italian villa or French chateau—when he could convince her. He heard her voice as he approached.

"I'll just have my things brought to this room if you're not using it."

"No, ma'am. I live with me children down in the servants' cottages."

"Very good. I will feel more comfortable here."

"If you are sure, miss," Cook said with uncertainty.

More comfortable? She wasn't comfortable?

"Yes, I am used to more modest accommodation, and it isn't proper for the housekeeper to be above stairs with the family," Gwen reassured Cook.

He could not stand to listen any longer. "Miss Lambert, may I have a word?"

She looked up and already had fire in her eyes. He was going to have to concentrate. She was magnificent.

"If you must."

"I'll just be getting back to me dough in the kitchen." Cook scooted out as quickly as she could before the dam burst.

"What do you mean by moving in here?" he demanded.

"I am here to keep house, and these are the housekeeper's rooms." She folded her arms and looked him straight in the eye.

"Says who?"

"Says Lady Easton," she said with a satisfied smirk.

Blast. "You are my guest. I'll not have you working!"

"Who are you to say? You yourself are working!" she retorted.

"It's different! And only to get back to England faster!"

"Then go. We should be able to manage now." Her green eyes flashed brilliantly.

"Gwen, please explain why you are doing this." He threw his hands up, dumbfounded.

"Suit yourself, but may we leave my room?"

"No." He folded his arms and planted himself against the door blocking the exit.

"No?"

"Only if you agree to stay upstairs."

"Why does it matter?"

"Because that is where you belong."

"This is preposterous. How can you say such a thing? I've no choice but to earn my living now, and I would appreciate it if you'd allow me to do so respectably."

"I didn't mean..." He ran his fingers through his hair in frustration. How could he make her understand?

"Have I been disrespectful to you?"

"Perhaps I misunderstood."

"Pardon?" What could she have possibly misunderstood? How had their perfectly amiable relationship gone so sour? And when had she become so spirited? He had to stop this nonsense. He was going mad. All he could think about was how beautiful she looked with her wild hair and her cheeks flushed. He was not making his point satisfactorily with words, so he stepped forward, took her face in his hands and lowered his face to hers and kissed her.

She froze and stood immobile. He pressed his lips to hers and fought to maintain control. He did not wish to frighten her, but he'd dreamt of this moment for months, and he would savour it. He wrapped his arms around her and wanted to hold tight forever. He showered sweet gentle kisses upon her face and neck until he felt her melt in his arms. He took that as a good sign, and placed her arms around him as he moved back towards her lips. She fit him perfectly as he knew she would. God had made this woman for him, and the world seemed as it should be when he was with her. She still was not participating, but she wasn't protesting either. He would show her how he felt, since he could not seem to tell her.

"Sir!"

"Ma'am?"

She slugged him as hard as she could. She actually packed a decent punch, but it was worth it. Her chest was heaving, her cheeks and lips rosy, and her hair was everywhere. She'd never looked better, and he'd never wanted a woman more.

"Where did you learn to hit like that?" he said appreciatively.

"My brother. He felt I might need to defend myself from any more unwanted advances. Now, please leave."

He stood there staring at her dreamily as she fumed. "Pardon?"

"I asked you to leave."

"But...we kissed." His shoulders dropped and he stared at her in disbelief.

She turned away.

"Gwen," he pleaded.

"It cannot happen again," she said quietly. "Now, please go."

~*~

Gwen had to leave. She could not remain in this house. For one, because she had thoroughly enjoyed his kiss. She had never experienced anything like it, and she revelled in his attentions. It had been months since she had any meaningful physical touch. And also, since she had arrived at the plantation practically throwing herself at his feet, she should expect him to behave in such a manner. Why could she not have stayed in England waiting for his return like a proper lady? Then she could have found out about his other relationship without placing herself in this untenable situation. She should have listened to the Dowager. Now her chance at any semblance of self-respect was gone. Mr Abbott had never promised anything other than friendship. The realisation and overwhelming disappointment she felt filled her with despair.

She avoided everyone for the rest of the day, and even took dinner in her room. She hoped they would accept her new position and not expect her to dine with them. She was exhausted from tossing and turning the entire night, stewing over the mess she had made for herself, and hurt at seeing the woman on Mr Abbott's arm the night before, not to mention trying to put his kiss out of her mind. She heard a knock on her door and immediately her heart began to pound in her chest. What if it was him? She was not ready to face him yet.

"Miss Lambert? Gwen? It's Lydia. May I come in?"

Gwen rose hastily and removed the chair she had placed under the doorknob and unlocked the door.

"Goodness! Were you expecting an invasion?" she teased.

Gwen flushed. "No, I..."

"I wanted to see what the matter was. I was upstairs with the children last night and missed dinner. Nathaniel informed me that you had moved down here and had taken dinner in your room." Lydia sat on the bed and patted for Gwen to join her.

"This is where I belong, ma'am."

Lydia creased her brow with concern. "Do you truly believe that?"

"I should never have come."

"Well, you are here. It does no good to dwell on it now. You need to decide what you want in here," she put her hand over her heart, "and do your best to attain it."

"It is not so simple. I've made a mull of it."

"Are you with child?" Lydia asked bluntly.

Gwen looked up with wide eyes. "I, I don't think so."

"Have you had relations with a man?"

Gwen continued to look at her with increasing terror. "Is a kiss relations?"

Lydia repressed a smile. "No, dear. You will know."

"Oh, thank God." Gwen let out a sigh of relief and began to play with a loose tendril of hair.

"Then you have not mulled it up. I was once in a similar situation, you know."

"I did not know," she said with surprise.

"I found myself with child, and Lord Fairmont had gone off with the Army. After six years, I decided to fight for what was best for me and our child. I even followed him to a different continent."

Tears welled in Gwen's eyes. Lydia took her hand.

"I do not deserve him. My family is disgraced and I have nothing to offer him."

"Do you think Mr Abbott cares for that? He does not need your money, or anyone else's. He is looking for more. He could have had any of those things many times over, had he chosen to do so."

"You do not think me wanton for following him here? Or does he? And what about the lady on his arm when we arrived?"

"I did not notice a woman. I certainly did not see any ladies. Perhaps you were too tired from the trip and were imaging things. I would not be concerned. As for him thinking you wanton, you are properly chaperoned, my dear. I think your heart led you here, and now you are torturing yourself with doubts. Did he give you cause to think he was not honourable?"

Gwen's cheeked pinked and she looked down.

"Other than a kiss?"

"I don't know."

"Then the choice is yours. From my point of view, and I've known him for years, you hold his heart in your hands." Lydia rose. "Now let us move you back upstairs where you belong and allow Josie to see to housekeeping duties."

Gwen opened her mouth to protest.

"You can still be useful in other capacities. I will need your help choosing draperies and furnishings for the new wing. And Amelia will be brokenhearted if she cannot have more lessons from you. I understand you are to paint River's Bend?"

Gwen knew she had been out-manoeuvred so she nodded. She had promised Lady Easton she would make her a painting.

"Very good. We will be leaving for church in an hour. Will you be joining us?"

"Yes, of course. Thank you, Lady Fairmont."

~*~

Gwen managed to ride in the carriage with the children to Christ's Church in Alexandria. It was a Palladian structure of golden stone which

187

made her unconsciously looked towards Mr Abbott, who was watching knowingly for her reaction. She could not help but smile appreciatively and longingly at the reminder of her old home. For a brief moment their eyes met, and she was tempted to run into his arms and beg him to take care of her however he saw fit.

"That will land you right at the Pearly Gates, I'm sure," Gwen muttered to herself.

No. He eventually would tire of her, and then what would become of her? She took a deep breath and looked upward towards the church's tower and beyond to the sky. Something about the sky always re-assured her, and she knew everything would turn out as it ought. She had no idea how, but it was not her place to worry, she tried to remind herself. She had been taken care of so far—even on the days when she'd been down to her last pence and piece of bread. Something had always turned up.

She looked back down when she heard a carriage drive up. One, two, three, four young ladies exited the carriage dressed in their Sunday finest, which was more suited to England's court dress. In a word, extravagantly.

She looked on with curiosity, then repulsion, as one of them stalked towards Mr Abbott like a hawk swooping in for its prey. Immediately she recognized the lady from the night they arrived. She knew she had not imagined it! Despite herself, she took her in dislike. Her instincts were normally quite astute. Except when it came to herself. She recalled her youthful naivety soon after her father's fall from grace. Several handsome suitors had paid her lavish attention and had sent her fine gifts. When she'd realised their intentions were not of an honourable nature, she'd been utterly humiliated and demoralised. Her brother had been around to advise her then. Now she had no one she felt like she could turn to, for no one truly understood her position. Lady Fairmont was kind and spoke of similarities...perhaps. But she was close friends with Mr Abbott. Josie was a kind soul, but she was not caught between classes as Gwen was.

The people were beginning to file into the church with *that woman,* as she now thought of her, still clinging to his arm. She attempted to place herself in a position where she would not have to watch, but she felt her arm being grasped and tucked into his body. She knew it was him without looking. He smelled of lemon and spice and man. Divine.

"You cannot avoid me forever."

"It would seem not."

"I will not apologise for kissing you either," he leaned over and whispered.

"I have not asked it of you."

"True, but you are angry. And while you are beautiful when you are angry, I prefer our easy friendship as before."

She wanted that too. But how? She wanted to believe Lady Lydia's words, but Mr Abbott's actions were not supportive of his affection for her, and only her.

"I do not think it possible, Mr Abbott. Now may we focus on worship?"

"May we call a truce first?"

"Certainly."

As if she would be able to concentrate when he wedged himself up against her in the pew. She sat stiff and rigid the entire sermon, desperately trying to keep from leaning into him. When the Reverend began by reading Matthew 19:19, her cheeks began to flush with chagrin. Her mind began to wander to the lady across the aisle, and Mr

Abbott's relationship with her, despite her best efforts to focus. She did not wish to be preached to about loving thy neighbour at that precise moment.

"Love thy neighbour as thyself. Being civil, doing no harm, taking a meal in times of sickness—these are all admirable traits. But they are not enough, my brethren. No, your heart must match your deeds. Deeds alone are not enough," the Reverend preached.

"Love as thou lovest thyself. If we all loved our neighbours as we loved our pugs and packs of hounds or our trusty steeds, what a better place the world would be!"

Indeed.

"Love is slow to anger. I do not pretend anger never happens, but be as quick to forgive others as one would forgive oneself."

Gwen could not forgive herself her own stupidity. Therein lay her problem.

"Love does not envy or treat others with disdain. We shall all die and return to dust, the pauper the same as the prince."

Amen. She hoped the *lady* on the other side of the aisle was listening.

"Love does not judge. Are you yourself without sin? Put yourself in your neighbour's shoes and ask how you can help him, instead of condemning him."

Father forgive me.

"If they reject thy love, if your acts of love are only returned with insult, remember 'tis not them you seek to please."

Rejected was apt for her love at the moment.

"I challenge you, my friends; treat others as you wish to be treated and you will find the path to happiness."

Gwen was not sure precisely how she wished to be treated, but *this* was not it.

"And finally, you may love yourself as much as you wish." This statement drew a chuckle from the crowd. "But remember to love your neighbour equally as much."

When at last the final hymn was sung Gwen was thankful to escape into the cool autumn air. Mr Abbott was following closely behind. She stopped and he nearly bumped into her.

"May I assist you with something?"

"I wanted to talk more."

"I do not think this the best place for a tête-à-tête."

The lady and her mother were making a beeline straight towards them. He stooped towards her and said, "Play along, please."

"Yoo-hoo, Mr Abbott!" the odious woman called out from under her equally obnoxious bonnet.

"Good day, Mrs Bradley." He bowed to acknowledge the mother. "Miss Bradley."

"Are you going to introduce us to your guests?"

"This is Miss Gwendolyn Lambert and Lord and Lady Fairmont, some of my family from England." "Mrs Bradley and Miss Bradley, our neighbours to the west."

"Oh!" Mrs Bradley pressed a hand up to her bountiful bosom. "Such an honour!" She attempted a curtsy to the Fairmonts as if they were royalty. It never failed to amuse Andrew. Unless it was directed at him. "We are having a dinner this week; we would be delighted to introduce you and welcome you to the neighbourhood."

"You are too kind, ma'am," Nathaniel replied civilly.

Mrs Bradley turned her gaze upon Gwen and her face turned shrewish as she examined her from head to toe.

"So this is the much exalted Miss Lambert."

"Indeed it is." Andrew stepped closer and took Gwen's hand.

"You did not appear to be very enamoured during church."

"It would hardly be the place, ma'am," Gwen could not help from remarking. She was uncertain why she should appear enamoured anyway, but she played along. There was an appreciative gleam on both Lord and Lady Fairmont's faces, and she had a hard time keeping her own face impassive. She had lost all patience for harpies after her treatment in Bath when her father died. However, the lady's face indicated she was declaring war.

"Indeed it would not. Good day Mr Abbott. Lord and Lady Fairmont. Come along, Jenny."

Jenny followed reluctantly, but looked back longingly several times.

"I do believe you have been snubbed, Miss Lambert," Andrew remarked amusedly. "I have not managed to achieve such a feat yet."

"It is quite simple. You have to want to be snubbed. Treat others as you wish to be treated." With that she turned and walked over to the carriage containing the children and climbed in. She glanced out the window to see Miss Bradley talking to Mr Abbott again. She leaned forward to listen.

"A lover's quarrel, Mr Abbott?"

"That is none of your concern, Miss Bradley."

"I would appreciate you properly, sir," she purred, and moved closer placing her hand on his arm.

"I've no doubt of that, ma'am." He smiled down at her, the rogue!

Then she boldly pulled him down and kissed him before running back to her carriage. She turned around and smirked at Gwen before the carriage pulled away. Gwen had never considered physically harming anyone before, but if she was ever close enough to *that woman* she would not answer for her actions. She might have to enlist Lady Easton's methods for world diplomacy. She could definitely foresee sketching that nasty smirk and rearranging it in a more fitting way. Surely God did not mean for her to love the spiteful, hateful Bradleys?

~*~

"Oh, Andrew, how could you do that to Gwen?" Lydia began chastising him before he had closed the door to the carriage.

He looked to Nathaniel for sympathy but there was none to be had.

Lydia continued, "We are not playing *ton* games here. She is not used to such, and nothing will turn her away faster. Society has not been kind to her and you would do well to remember that. Why did you allow Miss Bradley so close?"

"I was being neighbourly?" He shrugged.

"Even I could see that one coming," Nathaniel remarked, referencing his one eye.

"Honestly, my mind was on Miss Lambert and I was caught somewhat unawares. You don't suppose I could use it to my advantage?" Andrew asked sheepishly, knowing the answer. "What can I do?"

"You must tell her how you feel. I know it is not natural for a man, but I believe she does not think she is worthy, and I suspect she thinks your offer to be of a different nature."

"I never!"

"I know that, but does she?"

"Then why did she come all the way to America? If she was uncertain of my intentions, that is."

"She was urged on by Lord Kendall and Elly," Nathaniel answered.

"I know that when I chased Nathaniel to the Continent, I second-guessed myself a thousand times, if not more. I had convinced myself I would be content to live on my own with Amelia. And for a time I'd had no choice." Lydia teared up a bit at the recollection, and Nathaniel took her hand. "I suspect that Elly convinced her your intentions were honourable, but when she arrived she began to doubt."

"I've never been plainer in my life!"

"We all know that, Andrew. We can see that you were made for each other. But consider what she has been through. She is still grieving for her mother, whom she cared for on her own for six years. She now finds herself destitute and dependent on our family's charity. She leaves the only home she's ever known and finds herself in a strange land with no money or connections, should we decide to abandon her."

"She's terrified," he stated as if he finally understood.

"I believe so. She does not consider herself to be of our class, and cannot imagine why you would lower yourself, or what she could offer as your bride."

"But Kendall offered," Nathaniel pointed out.

"He hardly left her feeling worthy."

"I don't give a fig for any of that! I've no need to marry, and I don't need her money!"

"Then I suggest you convince her. And I would suggest you try with words first."

"After the look on her face when she saw you with Miss Bradley, you might have to be more creative," Nathaniel added dryly.

Andrew thrust his face into his hands. "Why must you ladies be so deuced complicated?"

"We would not want to bore you."

"Did I say I was bored?"

"Convince her that your sun rises and sets with her," Lydia advised.

"She's 'all that's best of dark and bright.'" Nathaniel added.

"I never knew you to be a poet, Nate."

"It's Byron. Perhaps it would behoove you to learn a little yourself."

"If only I was not acquainted with him."

~*~

Why had she come? And why had Mr Abbott put her in such a position? What had he told those people about her? Clearly he had said something. She felt hurt, jealous, angry, humiliated; there was nothing admirable about how she felt as she watched out the window on the return to the plantation. She had mistaken Mr Abbott's regard for her and felt the fool. He flirted with all ladies the same as he did with her!

She was going to have to return to England. It was clear she would not be welcomed here. She would start on the painting for Elly immediately. She would beg the Fairmonts if she had to—offer Amelia art lessons for life if necessary for her passage fare if they were not ready to return. It was too painful to be near Mr Abbott. She could never be the type of woman that looked the other way.

She should have controlled her reaction to that harpy and not let her see her anger. She should have said something cleverer. She was certain it would come to her later. She had never had the gift of a quick tongue. A quick temper, yes. She certainly had the redheaded fire in her blood.

The carriage pulled up to the house. Josie and Buffy helped the children out of the carriage. Gwen followed and passed through the kitchen on the way to her room and asked for a small lunch to take with her. She intended to complete as much of the picture as possible today.

She packed up her sketching supplies and a hamper of food, avoiding the main staircase and anywhere she thought he might be. Outdoors, she went in search of the perfect spot. Once she had the sketch she could find somewhere else to paint. She looked about for a place she could draw in relative privacy unseen from the house.

Unfortunately, the best view would be in a boat on the river. She was not about to suggest such a thing to Mr Abbott. Who knew what he might try once he had her alone out there? She thought of their kiss, and then what she had witnessed with Miss Bradley. Apparently kisses were given out as readily as comfits at Christmas by Mr Abbott, she thought angrily. *Love thy neighbour indeed*!

She settled near a tree by the landing. She opened the hamper and ate some food while she studied the house from the front façade. That was the angle both Lord and Lady Easton were most fond of.

The square bold lines of the house with its thick pillared columns took form quickly on the pad, each stroke venting some of her anger onto the page. She added in the curve of the river and then the surrounding trees. As her frustration faded into her work, she decided it would be best to act like nothing had happened, and that she was unaffected.

She was not at all good at masking her emotions, but it would be necessary to try to further protect her heart. That it was already broken she could not deny. It did not mean she wanted it injured further. The worst part was, she had no one to be angry with but herself. Mr Abbott had promised her nothing.

She sat back and compared her drawing with the real thing. She had decided upon everything except the sky. The sky had been crystal clear that morning as they had gone to church. But now the clouds were unlike any she had ever seen before. They stretched out in a pattern as if a bird had spread its wing and was wrapping it around the sky.

Perhaps tomorrow the sky would be better, although the sunset held glorious hues of pinks, violets and ambers. She could decide as she slept. She often dreamt of scenes in paintings. The air was growing more humid, so she gathered up her things and returned to the house.

"There you are," Lady Fairmont exclaimed. "We were about to send a search party out for you."

"I apologise. I was frustrated, and I wanted to sketch out the painting for Lady Easton."

"I assumed it was something of the sort, but convincing Andrew that you were unharmed was more difficult."

"I was only by the landing." What right did he have to be concerned?

"Well, you look like you are intact. Shall I fetch someone to help you dress for dinner?"

"Perhaps help with my hair."

"I'll send Josie. We will wait for you in the drawing room. We are to dine at the neighbours'."

"Lady Fairmont?" Gwen called after her.

"Yes?"

"When do you think you will be returning to England?"

"We have made no plans as of yet. Is everything all right?"

"I think it best that I return with you," Gwen said quietly.

Lady Fairmont's face softened. "Then I shall inform you when we have plans. You are of course welcome to come with us."

"Thank you."

Gwen sighed and went to change. She wished she had been bold enough to beg. She could not avoid Mr Abbott forever. She wished she were not so affected by his presence. She had spun fantastic tales in her mind about them knowing they were ridiculous unreality. The sooner she was away from him the better.

Chapter Sixteen

Gwen had lost her mind. She could not trust her judgment or counsel. She was receiving confusing signals from every front. Lady Fairmont had said they were to dine with the neighbours. She had not realised which neighbours. She had politely demurred when informed, thinking her mourning state a proper excuse. She was reassured it was only a small dinner, with no dancing.

Lady Fairmont pulled her aside. "We could make your excuses, but that would allow the Bradleys an entire evening to avail themselves of Andrew," she said in a hushed voice to avoid being overheard.

"I do not see that is any business of mine," Gwen said as politely as she could.

"Very well. I understand your sentiments. I cannot say I would feel any differently." Lady Fairmont replied. "But did you come this far to give up so easily?"

"It is not a matter of giving up. It is more his behaviour towards other women which leaves me to feel I am out of place."

"I believe there has been some gross misunderstanding. Unless you have had a change of heart?" Lady Fairmont searched Gwen's face.

Gwen shook her head.

"Then may I suggest you postpone your judgement a bit longer and give him another chance. And if you mean to win him for yourself you best make it your concern and attend the dinner," Lady Fairmont said quietly with a wink and an encouraging squeeze of her hand. "Men are literal creatures, Gwen. You must be very plain to them and not expect them to guess at your thoughts." With that advice she walked away as

Mr Abbott approached.

"Gwen. Please come. I know you are angry with me, but we can have dinner with friends, surely."

She looked sideways at him with narrowed eyes.

"Very angry. I confess I might have hinted we were betrothed and it would look odd were you not to attend."

Gwen's heart leapt from her chest, but the words she had longed to hear were bittersweet.

"Why would you say such a thing?"

"I was attempting to deter some of the ambitious mamas."

That was not the answer she wanted to hear. She wanted to believe his affection for her was reciprocated, but the signs were not convincing.

"Please. We can discuss this later, but can we pretend for tonight?"

Pretend. He wanted her to pretend. She stood there, assimilating his words with Lady Fairmont's. She wanted to be furious and throw something. The irony of the situation only made her furious with her own poor judgement. She had come here with the hope of becoming his wife, only to find him making up to other women, or at least not discouraging their advances. It made the offence more grievous to her knowing he behaved this way, and all the while the town had thought him engaged. Making a May game of her was how it felt. She did not want to go to a dinner and pretend anything. But she decided to heed Lady Fairmont's advice and reserve judgement for the time being.

"Very well. I will go."

She sat next to him in the carriage brooding while they rode to the Bradleys' welcoming soirée. The entire party was quiet, not knowing how Miss Lambert would choose to respond publicly to Andrew's decree. The fact that she was obliged to go to the home of the family that was the main source of her irritation was enough to send her Titian-headed temper into full swing. She debated how to go on as they pulled through the gates. She should act to the manor born and depress any pretentions the biddy Bradley proffered. Gwen was to the manor born, but as they drove up before a mansion as grand as River's Bend, her heart sank. The truth was, she no longer belonged to that world and did not know if she had the talent to pull off the charade. She had no idea how American society got on. She had never had the talent to pretend she was feeling other than she was—which at this moment was acutely vexed and deeply hurt. She did not know if she could trust him again, even if there was a misunderstanding.

"Well my dear, what shall it be?" Andrew braved her wrath.

Lady Fairmont spoke up, "I admit I cannot like the situation nor the circumstances, but you must admit it best to go along with the scheme while we are here, and not give the cat an opportunity to sink her claws into him."

"Yes, please do not leave my side," Andrew begged.

Gwen glared at him. He could have resolved this himself if he was truly repulsed by her, but as angry as she was, the thought of Miss Bradley in his arms was enough to firm her resolve. At least for the night.

"If you will not do it for Andrew, Miss Lambert, please do it for our sake," Lord Fairmont said in his usual sardonic manner.

"Pretend you're a duchess, dear," Lady Fairmont whispered into her ear as they alighted from the carriage. "Above all, do not show your emotion on your face."

Mr Abbott held out his arm to her and flashed his most charming smile. She took his arm reluctantly, knowing she would have difficulty not succumbing to his charms when he was so near. They entered the mansion and Gwen already felt herself disadvantaged at the stark reminder and contrast to her own situation. She was an impostor and she had not been in schooled in the arts of deception or pretending. She did not wish to be as haughty or pretentious as those as she sought to fool, but there again, it would be delicious to have the small victory.

"If you so much as smile at her, I will walk out," she warned Andrew through her smiling teeth.

"Agreed, my lady. I will do my best Lord Fairmont impression."

Lord Fairmont chuckled appreciatively.

They were shown into a large drawing room that was surprisingly filled with many unknown faces. Gwen instinctively shrank back, and Andrew leaned over and whispered reassurances into her ear as the Bradleys caught sight of the River's Bend party and came forward to greet them.

"Welcome!" Mr Bradley said jovially, and shook hands with Andrew.

"Thank you, Mr Bradley. May I present to you Miss Lambert?"

"I'm very pleased to meet you. I did not have the pleasure of making your acquaintance at church."

Gwen was thankful for Mr Bradley's pleasant manner and almost felt sorry for the man. He was clearly not the one who wore the breeches in his family.

"Thank you for having me, sir."

"Oh, we enjoy showing everyone southern hospitality, as they say. You are very welcome. I hope you enjoy your stay here."

Unfortunately they were required to greet the rest of the family too. Gwen hoped they did not expect to shake hands.

She stood tall and prepared for the assault. She followed Lady Fairmont's lead and kept her hands to herself, performing a slight curtsy when presented to Mrs and the Misses Bradley. They were too in awe of a real English lady to do anything but imitate her. Gwen made a note to watch Lydia more closely. Of course, Lady Fairmont was already married and was a grand lady.

She had felt the stares as they had made their way into the drawing room. She'd had the luxury of hiding her hair under a bonnet at church. Even though Josie had contrived to tame her mane, the humidity now caused her locks to have a mind of their own. She should be used to this, but hiding away for six years had allowed her to forget for the most part. She knew she looked well in black, and she had on an elegant silk of Lady Easton's which was ornamented with silver around the bodice and skirt. She was wearing her mother's pearls, and had felt confident when she had left her bedroom, but now she wanted to shrink behind the drapery.

"Have I mentioned how beautiful you look?" Andrew said in her ear.

"No. Thank you." She fingered her pearls doubtfully.

"Your hair is especially...glorious." He looked at it admiringly.

"Pardon? Then why do they stare at me so?"

"They have never seen anything so beautiful, I imagine."

She could not help but roll her eyes at him.

"There is no need to poke fun."

"You might try to smile and act as though you adore me if you intend to convince Miss Bradley. She has been watching you like a hawk."

Gwen struggled not to turn and glare at her.

Meanwhile, Andrew took her hand and kissed it lovingly with hungry eyes. She struggled not to blush.

"If you keep looking at me that way, people will have no doubt of your intentions."

"That is the idea." He smiled, not to be deterred. Insufferable man.

"I do not intend to be feasted upon in the garden!" she reprimanded.

"Where did you have in mind?" he asked innocently.

She was speechless.

"Please, tell me you can appreciate a jest? I was only attempting to flirt."

"I am not practiced at flirtations," she retaliated.

"Very well, I shall instruct you. You simply smile, say witty things and rap my arm with your fan."

"Why on earth would I do such a thing?"

"It does look silly, I'll admit, but it is the way ladies converse in Society."

Gwen looked about and saw what he said to be true.

"Very well." She took her fan and smiled coquettishly.

He fought off the urge to laugh but his eyes twinkled. He nodded encouragement.

She boldly snapped her fan together against her hand and rapped his arm with gusto.

"Oh, Mr Abbott! That was exhilarating. I do think I might enjoy this after all."

"You are certainly a quick study," he said, rubbing the welt he was certain was forming on his arm.

~*~

Dinner was announced, and Mr Bradley asked Lord and Lady Fairmont to do the honours and lead the guests into dinner. Andrew took Miss Lambert's arm and led her into the dining room. But when it was time to be seated, Mrs Bradley directed him to sit next to Miss Bradley. He had been too well-trained in politeness not to sit where he was told, but it was with great foreboding and reluctance that he did so. He could sense Gwen's hesitation as he let go of her arm.

She looked like a goddess descended to Earth, resplendent in her gown. She outshone everyone in the room and it pained him to release her. He would spend his evening of torment watching her from the other end of the table whilst enduring the blatant advances of the Bradleys. He caught her look of scorn towards Miss Bradley and hoped he would be able to show Gwen she had nothing to be jealous about. He watched with relief as she was seated near Nathaniel. He would protect her, no doubt. Now could he protect himself and set Miss Bradley straight without offending her or Miss Lambert?

Whatever happened, he would not smile.

"Good evening, Mr Abbott," Miss Bradley said smoothly.

Her chair was already too close for comfort, and the first course had not been set out.

"Good evening, Miss Bradley," he said civilly, but did not smile. Being curt and pompous was not his nature, but if it meant losing Gwen...he unconsciously glanced again to where she sat at the end of the table.

"How long does she intend to stay?" Miss Bradley cast her eyes towards Gwen.

"As long as I do." He hoped that was true.

"And how long will that be?"

"I plan to sail in early spring. We've only ten rooms to finish, and that should be plenty of time."

"I see." She pouted. Lord help him through the dinner. "Well, then, I've still time to change your mind."

Ignoring her he said, "Lord Easton, Elly's husband, has sent his trusted man to take over as steward, so there will be no need for my presence any longer. There probably is no need for me now, but I'd like to see the job finished, even though I am not the owner of River's Bend," he said pointedly, hoping that would convince her to cease her shameless attentions.

"That is a terrible shame."

Miss Bradley scooted closer and batted her eyelashes. The soup tasted like refuse in Andrew's mouth.

"I'm certain I can convince you to stay."

He felt a foot creeping up his leg and her hand came to rest on his. He tried to pull it away but she held tight. He was afraid to look down the table. "Miss Bradley, this is hardly appropriate," he tried to mutter quietly. "I would appreciate it if you would allow me to have my hand back. It is most difficult to cut one's food single-handedly."

"Oh, silly me. I had not realised I was holding your hand!"

She continued to drop things and bend towards him to retrieve them throughout several courses, brushing up against him at every opportunity. It was going to be the longest night of his life. He never thought he would wish himself back in the Army, but he had not been trained for this type of battle. Most females took hints—subtle or not— and maintained a modicum of self-respect.

~*~

How long would she be subjected to this? Gwen was thankful she was not having to sit near Miss Bradley and Andrew while they flirted at least. It would not have surprised her had she been placed directly across from the display. She was listening to the men discuss storms with one ear, while wishing she could toss wine in Miss Bradley's smug face. She focused on appearing as if she was enjoying herself and trying not to run from the room. Her head was beginning to ache, and she was thinking

Scotland might be the place for her after all.

"The servants are convinced that a big storm is coming," Mr Bradley remarked.

"And why do they think that?" Lord Fairmont asked.

"I suppose it comes from years of living near the coast. Some say the air feels different, and another says you can tell by the clouds."

Gwen had noticed changes in both of those things earlier.

"I think they may be right. I felt the air grow more humid as I was sketching, and I noticed the clouds took on a strange pattern as well," she remarked.

"We are subject to strong gales along the coast, or hurricanes as some call them," Mr Bradley informed the dinner party.

"We've never had a hurricane affect us in Sussex that I remember," Lord Fairmont said, trying to recall.

"Perhaps Sussex is more protected being on the Channel, rather than the Atlantic Ocean, but I've read of some significant storms on other parts of the coast where the shore was rearranged," Gwen added.

"I'm sure that is true. I've heard sailors say much the same," he agreed.

"Will we be safe in the house?" Lady Fairmont asked from across the table, growing concerned.

"I believe so, but River's Bend is closer to the main river. We are further up the inlet here," Mr Bradley said thoughtfully.

"How long until the storm hits?" Gwen wondered.

"It could be a day or two. These storms move slowly and there will be a lot of wind and rain."

"That doesn't sound unbearable." She could always finish the painting inside if necessary.

"The main worry is the flooding. The servants are working as we speak to shore up some of the fields that are prone to holding water. Thankfully, the harvest is past, but a flood will put us back for planting. We have already moved the horses and livestock to higher ground. I will advise Mr Abbott to do the same, though I imagine Abe has it well in hand. After that, we wait for the storm to pass."

"Hopefully it will change direction and do little more than rain." Lord Fairmont spoke what they all wished.

Gwen heard very little of the rest of the conversation. She tried to ignore the insulting scene from the other end of the table, but she was only human. She needed to finish her painting and leave. As the talk of the storm grew, Mr Abbott became involved in the conversation and decided it best to leave early and make certain Abe was taking precautions. Never had Gwen been so thankful for an impending storm.

She kept to herself in the carriage on the ride back to the plantation. No one pressed her to talk—there was no need. All of them had been witnesses to the despicable scene at the dinner table. Gwen could not particularly say that Mr Abbott had reciprocated Miss Bradley's blatant advances, but again, he had not discouraged them.

She said a civil goodnight and hurried up to her chamber. She would rise early on the morrow to work on the picture. Perhaps she would capture a gloriously unique sky from the storm—a storm fit to match her mood.

~*~

She felt a nudge and opened one eye.

"Miss Lambert, tis early morning. You asked me to wake ye if I didn't see ye. I think it's a bad idea though, miss."

"Thank you, Cook," Gwen said sleepily. "No need to worry. I plan to return before the storm hits." She threw back her counterpane and went over to push the curtains aside. It was still dark. She dressed, and then hurried with her things outside. She intended to paint at the summer house on the other side of the creek. She could paint in her room, but she had always preferred to paint outdoors. It was more inspiring to be amongst Nature.

If there was to be a storm, she should be safe there. Rain and wind was all they had predicted. It was further up the property from the river anyway. She loaded her easel and canvas into the back of a cart and found one of the workers to drive her. It was not very far, but the easel was more than half her weight.

As she rode the short distance, she looked skyward and saw the clouds were thick, circular and moving in one direction. As the dawn began to break, she grew excited for capturing the storm's effect on these unusual clouds. The air was sticky and there was a wind beginning to blow. It was an eerie feeling, but she hastened those thoughts aside with her excitement to paint. The summer house was a quaint cottage with a covered porch. That would be perfect from whence to view and attempt to capture Nature's magnificence.

The worker helped her unload the easel and canvas and place them on the porch. Cook had sent a large hamper of food, fearing Gwen would get caught out by the weather and be obliged to wait. Gwen had thought it ridiculous, but did not argue. She was not even a mile from the manor house and there were servants' cottages everywhere around. She could walk that far in the rain if necessary. She donned an apron and prepared to work. She prepped her canvas and made the outline for the house. She studied the sky and began mixing pigments to capture the unique cloud and colour formations the storm was causing.

The clouds grew angry and fierce as they swirled, and looked as if they were coming towards the Earth to engulf them. She had always enjoyed thunderstorms with brilliant lightning and strong smells—things she could not capture on canvas. Rain she was more than accustomed to, living in the wettest town in England. Deluge threatened in heavy dark clouds and sprinkles of rain began to fall. It was like nothing she had ever seen before, and she had seen a lot of rain clouds in Somerset.

She painted furiously and began to wonder when the cart would return for her as the winds began to howl and the rain poured in sheets. She carried her picture to safety inside and watched out of the window, hoping she had not been forgotten in all of the storm preparation. She should not have insisted on painting this morning, or at least not so far away. She could think of little else after that insulting episode at dinner last night. Now that her temper was subdued she began to worry.

The rain continued to fall, and Gwen pondered walking back. She could return for the painting later. It would be ruined if she were to attempt to carry it. She had only accomplished the sky thus far. She decided to have a bite to eat, and then she would set out on foot if they had not come for her by the time she'd finished painting.

~*~

Andrew was aching from head to toe. He and all the men had worked the entire night in the fields to prepare for the likelihood of flooding. He was not sure how any of their efforts would make a difference if enough water fell from the sky and the river rose over its banks. He had nevertheless decided to heed Abe's warnings and ordered all of the servants to higher ground at the manor house. He was responsible for many lives and he would take every precaution. The Army had taught him: things can be replaced, people cannot.

He decided to take a quick rest before the storm hit. He woke to the sound of rain beating a harsh drumming on the window. He recalled the circumstances and shot up from the bed to look out. There was little visibility, but the trees were being blown about and the rain appeared to be coming down sideways.

He splashed water on his face and straightened his clothing, before rushing out to check on the status of things. The house was crowded, for he had ordered everyone to wait out the storm here. Fortunately the wing under construction was advanced enough at this point that the rooms were habitable. Still, it was crowded with over two hundred people inside. He went in search of Buffy and Nathaniel to see if there were any last-minute necessities. They had also worked the entire night and had to be as exhausted as he. Even though he was responsible for River's Bend, they shared the burden equally as they would have on the battlefield. He had never known he would be so grateful for his Army training—or find it useful—in retirement.

He passed through the great hall which had been turned into a makeshift nursery for all of the children. The older children had lively game of rounders going on, and he chuckled as Amelia was organising the lot of them. They were using a candlestick as a bat, and he had to duck to miss a ball flying at his head. She was so much like Elly he hoped Nathaniel was prepared when she entered Society!

He passed through into the library where he was certain to find the men, but it was abandoned at present, save for a map of the properties spread out on the table. He took a glance at it himself, which was pointless, since he had learned every inch of the land over the past months. He heard the wind howling and the rain pouring, and was grateful he had heeded Abe's advice. The servants' cottages were too close to the river should it rise and flood.

He said a quick prayer that the storm would pass quickly. Abe told him that several years past one storm had stalled and remained for a week. The fields certainly would not stand a chance, and how far would the river rise if that happened? The manor house was on a hill of sorts, but it was not impervious to a high rushing tide.

He needed to find the men. He wanted to account for every person. He walked on through the house and ended up at the kitchen. Cook was busy preparing food for the unexpected mouths she would be feeding.

"Good afternoon, Mr Abbott."

"Hello, Cook. Can you tell me where everyone has gone? I cannot find any of the men."

A look of guilt passed over Cook's face. She was clearly hiding something from him.

"What is it? It would be better to tell me now," he said in his Army commander voice.

"I'm not sure of that now."

He kept staring at her. He knew from years of experience people would eventually talk.

"They's gone after Miss Lambert," she muttered quietly.

"And where has Miss Lambert gone that they have felt the need to go after her?" he said with every ounce of composure he could muster when his insides were churning.

"She left before dawn to paint at the summer house. She was muttering about glorious clouds and capturing them."

Blast! Forget composure.

"She promised to return before the rain started, or I would never have let her go," she said defensively.

"How long ago did they set out?"

"'Bout an hour ago when the rain got fierce. Abe was wanting to check on the river, and Lord Fairmont suggested accounting for everybody. Jim asked where she be and if someone'd fetched 'er. I got so busy cooking in here that I forgot to send someone after her like I promised. I am very sorry, sir." Cook's eyes welled up with tears and shame. "Six of 'em went after 'er."

"Let us pray that they get her returned before the bridge washes out."

"Oh, lawks! Lord have mercy! I'd not thought of the bridge!"

"I'm off to help. Keep everyone inside. Do whatever you have to do to keep them there."

"Yessir. I'll do me best."

~*~

Andrew felt the agony of anticipation as he rushed outside into the storm. Like when he knew his first pony would have to be put down, when he knew his mother was going to die, or when he thought Nathaniel gone. But this was different. He had only unrequited love for Gwendolyn. And he could not bear the thought of never knowing, sharing, holding...one taste had not been enough. He ran faster, struggling against the fierce winds, praying he was not too late, that he would run into the men, all of them rain and weather-beaten but unharmed.

But where were they? He should have found them by now. He could barely make out his nose on his face, but he was certain he'd gone the proper direction. A bolt of lightning flashed, and an old beech tree cracked and began its decent downward. He stopped to catch his breath and check his surroundings, thankful for the small favour of missing the tree by seconds. He heard rushing water between the thunder and gusts of wind. Another flash of lightning showed him to be amongst the servants' cottages. The bridge had to be to his left. He walked along the creek, now overflowing its banks, looking for the crossing. There could not be much time left for the small bridge, if it was still standing.

At last he came upon the men standing at the bridge, which was being stripped of its pieces as they watched.

"Where is she?" Andrew shouted.

"She's still over there." Nathaniel pointed towards the cottage. "We were afraid to chance the bridge. She is safer inside," he yelled over the wind and water.

"We cannot leave her alone!" Andrew exclaimed. "The water could overtake the cottage if it continues at this rate!"

"That bridge is not safe to cross. I could not ask it of her, or the men," Nathaniel reasoned loudly. "We must get to safety ourselves. She'll be all right, Andrew!"

"You go! I'll not leave her!"

Andrew ran towards the bridge and began to cross before anyone could stop him, holding on to the remaining pieces of the frame.

"Andrew! No!" Nathaniel called after him.

Andrew yelled without looking back, "You would do the same!"

All of the men held their breath as he lost his footing and fell into the water. When his head reappeared, he gasped for breath, but he was holding on to the rail with rushing water beneath his chin.

Both Buffy and Nathaniel had begun to strip off their jackets and boots to go after him, when Andrew managed to begin moving along the rail by swinging one arm forward at a time.

Gwen had been watching from the porch and ran towards him screaming, "No!"

He moved with more purpose at the sight of her, though it was a struggle to grasp the rail with the force of the river pushing against him. He still had a few feet left and he was growing tired.

"You can make it!" he heard a voice shout.

"Just a little further, Andrew!" he heard Nathaniel yell.

"Don't you dare leave me, you insufferable impossible oaf!"

That was music to his ears. He smiled through the pain and pressed forward another arm's length. She was bent over holding out her hand to him. As much as he longed to grasp it, he knew it would only serve to pull her in. He needed to find a way to thrust himself upwards without harming her. He felt the force of the water pulling the bridge from behind him. He did not have long until the rest of the structure was swept away.

Gwen seemed to understand the predicament, and she ran over to the porch. She came back struggling with the weight of her easel and placed it on the ground within reach and sat on the opposite end while holding on to a tree. It was doubtful it would work, but he had little choice but to try.

He swept one arm out and made contact. The hold was a difficult one that he would not be able to maintain for long. He could already feel it sliding in the muddy bank.

"Come on, I can't hold this for long," she shouted. He took a deep breath and let go of the bridge. She had turned over on to her stomach and had her legs wrapped around the tree. He could see her pain as she exerted all of her strength to pull him out. He moved slowly forward and tried to find his footing on the bank. He managed a small toe-hold and pushed his body with every ounce of strength he had.

He felt the wind knocked out of him as his chest hit the easel. He was already beginning to slide backwards and quickly recovered so as to not lose the ground he had gained.

"Don't let go! I'm almost there," he shouted.

"Hurry, please! I cannot feel my legs! I'm not certain if I am still holding onto the tree."

By the grace of God he was able to thrust his legs up onto the remaining ground.

He heard shouts from across the river and he gave a slight wave from his prone position.

"Get inside!"

He wobbled as he found his feet, then grabbed Gwen's hand and began running towards the cottage.

On the porch he began stripping off his wet clothes and boots. It would have been much easier without those, he thought in retrospect.

Gwen had turned her back. He laughed to himself. She was stuck with him forever, so he hoped she'd enjoyed her preview.

"I'll go and fetch blankets, then you must get out of your wet clothes, too."

"I think not."

"You mean I risked my life, only to let you die of lung fever? *I* think not. A soldier learns quickly to lose his modesty or his life."

He stormed into the cottage and returned wrapped in a toga-like concoction.

He dramatically slid towards her backwards holding out a blanket to her.

She grabbed it forcefully out of his hands.

"Now hurry."

"Yes, sir!" She mimicked a soldier obeying orders, and he could just see her mock saluting him behind his back.

Chapter Seventeen

Gwen walked into the cottage and found Mr Abbott wringing his wet clothes and laying them out to dry. He then began building a fire in the hearth with the few dry pieces of wood they had.

She'd covered herself up to her chin with the blanket he'd provided to her, and sat in a chair remaining silent and completely unnerved. She did not know how she felt, nor what to say. She was still shaking with fright from fear of watching him almost swept away by the raging current.

He built the fire with purpose, acting relaxed—as if he hadn't almost died.

"Where are your clothes?" he asked as he positioned the wood. "We need to dry them, for we might need them again soon. I'm afraid it won't be a restful night. We have to keep an eye on the river rising," he said as he bent down to light the tinder.

She could not help but notice how handsome he was as she watched him work.

"I spread them out on the porch. They were covered in mud."

He went out on to the porch and was gone a few minutes. She began to worry when he came back in wringing out her wet clothes and shaking his wet head. His blanket was dry…

She must have looked confused.

"I had to wash the mud out. Unfortunately, the creek is overrunning the banks by a few feet already. If the rain doesn't let up, we will be on the roof soon."

"The roof? In this storm?"

"If it comes to it. I won't stay in here and drown when I can take my chances up there."

She watched him in astonishment, wondering how he could remain so calm.

"If only I'd eaten dinner before, this would not be such an unpleasant arrangement."

How could he think of food right now? She had a hard time looking at him dressed in the blanket and not staring, so she kept her eyes averted to the fire. She looked up momentarily and told him about the remains of the hamper of food that Cook had sent.

He happily trudged towards the hamper, exclaiming at the amount of food still left. "There is enough food here for a week! This isn't so bad, then." He began fortifying himself with a chicken leg. "Would you care for anything?"

She didn't want to think about food, or anything but how to maintain sanity while in a small cottage with the man she loved, who thought nothing of kissing and flirting with other women.

"You cannot stay angry with me forever." He held out a plum as a peace-offering. When had he come so close?

She stared at the plum, but didn't move. "I can if I like." She turned her head away. He would not be let off the hook so easily. She tried very hard to stay angry, but he refused to be put off.

"I'm sorry." He was close. His gaze was disconcerting, and full of consternation.

"For what?" she prodded, breaking his intense gaze.

"You are the one who is angry, and I must spell it out?"

"I want to make sure you understand fully what I am angry about."

"For letting that encroaching arch-wife and her daughter near me." He threw his hands up. "This is ridiculous!"

"You expected me to believe your intentions towards me are honourable after I saw you with that…*that harpy*? I have no intention of being a woman that looks the other way."

"I did not encourage her to behave so."

"You did not discourage her."

"What was I supposed to do?"

"Tell her, no thank you? Spit in her face?"

He gurgled laughter. "You're more spirited than you led me to believe."

"Jonathan Swift warned you. Or did you not say that you'd read the book? She quoted, '*It is observed that the red-haired of both sexes are more…*' She paused, omitting the word 'libidinous', but blushed anyway. '*…Mischievous than the rest, whom yet they much exceed in strength and activity.*'"

"You left out a word. And my favourite part," he said with a sly grin.

"You are proving my point."

"How is that?"

She cast him a look of exasperation. When she received a blank stare in return, she shook her head. He had no idea.

"I don't know what to do." She shook her head and resolved to remain strong, despite the fact that she felt some otherworldly pull to him; she could not allow herself to give in.

"Why won't you let me take care of you?" He knelt down before her at eye level, his expression guarded, his eyes confused.

"I could not live with my conscience!" she blurted out.

"I see." He stood and turned away.

They heard a loud crack and a tree came crashing through the window, shattering it and sending shards of glass flying in every direction.

~*~

Nathaniel and the men had a difficult time making their way back to the house through the storm. Trees were down everywhere and the rain was soaking the ground up to their ankles, making walking a challenge for five disabled veterans with varying injuries. When they finally arrived, they were wet through and exhausted. However, they were not to have time to rest. They could hear the household in chaos when they closed the front door. The winds were howling, the shutters were rattling, and Cook and Josie were shouting orders louder than Wellington's finest.

Nathaniel surveyed the scene: the army of servants hauling furniture and food stores to dry ground; the women hauling children up the stairs. It was difficult to see clearly by candlelight. He attempted to move forward and join in the efforts, but when he moved his feet were heavy and resistant. He looked down to see a sludge of mud covering his boots. Only one thing was certain—they would not be leaving for England any time soon.

"What can we do to help? Where is Lady Fairmont?" he asked.

"She is handling the children upstairs. The great room is flooding. We need more lanterns and, of course, help saving as much of the food as we can," Josie explained.

Abe went off looking for the lanterns, and the other men joined together in an assembly line, passing what stores of food from the larder that could be salvaged.

Buffy and Nathaniel made their way through to see that the children were safe and no injuries needed attending to.

"How much longer will this last?" Nathaniel asked.

"I've no idea." Abe said, "Usually no more than a day. But sometimes it can be near a week."

The storm had been producing rain for over twelve hours. The fierce winds had been raging for several. Nathaniel had no idea how they would manage for days with the river flowing through the house. He hoped the foundations would hold until the water receded. It would be madness trying to manage two hundred servants and children in this mess if they survived, but he had lived through worse. It was eerily similar to some of the experiences on the Peninsula, save for the heavy numbers of women and children he was responsible for here.

They managed to salvage most of the food stores, thanks to Cook and Josie's quick actions. The women were doing their best to calm the children and put the anxious ones to sleep. The men had done all they could to secure the house and everyone was accounted for, save Andrew and Miss Lambert. He said a quick prayer for their safety, but their fate was out of his control. When the rain stopped, he would send a boat for them and hope the cottage had stood fast.

"Mr Abbott?" Gwen asked worriedly as she nudged the heavy body on top of her and heard a slight groan. "Sir, are you hurt?"

"Miss Lambert? Is that you?"

"Yes," she replied warily.

"Have I died and gone to heaven?"

"I do not believe so. What would make you think such a thing?" she asked in disbelief.

"I've dreamt for months about this very thing," he said in a cheeky voice.

"I am certainly delighted to know your dreams have been fulfilled, but I am having a hard time breathing and am acutely uncomfortable," she retorted.

"Beg pardon." He scrambled up. "Why didn't you say so sooner?"

"I thought you might be hurt," she replied.

"No. I don't think I am, only a little dazed."

"Tackling persons occasionally has that effect," she said sarcastically, which she knew he would appreciate.

"I was trying to protect you," he said with a twinkle in his eyes.

"Thank you." Her cheeks grew warm at the tender look he gave her. He helped her up, then walked gingerly over shards of glass that were strewn everywhere, to stoke the fire in order to provide more light in the room.

"Amazing how much glass comes from one window," he remarked as he looked around. "We should probably retrieve our boots from the porch. It is not safe to walk in here." He tiptoed through the glass towards the door to find their boots.

Gwen agreed as she scanned the small cottage. Rain was blowing in through the broken window, they were wearing makeshift togas, and she had risked several lives because of her stupidity. She teared up, and felt even more helpless and lost. She was thankful Mr Abbott was safe, and if they lived through this awful storm, she only hoped he would forgive her.

She heard him rummaging through closets and cupboards, and then he presented himself in his muddied top boots holding a broom and her shoes. He grinned at her, set her shoes before her, and began to sweep up the glass.

"This is rather fun," he said as he gathered the glass into a pile.

"Not when you are obliged to do it every day for a living," she remarked.

"No, I suppose it wouldn't be."

"How did it look outside?"

"A bit calmer, though the water is much closer now. I recommend we try to rest while we can. I suspect the adventure is not yet behind us."

"I suppose not, though I've no experience with hurricanes. I'd no idea rain and wind could continue at this pace for so long."

"I've been in some bad storms, but this certainly goes beyond imagination. You take the bed, I'll sleep here," he ordered.

"That is not necessary. I'm smaller, I shall sleep here."

"Miss Lambert, do not be difficult."

"I'm being practical," she insisted.

"Certainly. Then I will be forced, as a gentleman, to take the floor, and that means I will need to put a blanket on the floor and the only ones available are around you and me. That will leave the perfectly comfortable bed unused, and my person in my God-given skin. It matters not to me, I was used to sleeping in such conditions when I was in the army." He folded his arms and shrugged.

"Gentlemen's rules are what killed my father. I've no use for them. If you insist on stupidity, enjoy the floor." She turned away from him and positioned herself on the small sofa. She let out an involuntary shriek of pain and Mr Abbott was instantly by her side.

"What is the matter? Are you hurt? Let me look!"

He began to fuss over her, checking for any signs of injury.

"The pain was in my shoulder. It is likely only a small shard of glass."

He pulled her forward and looked at the back of her shoulder. He was quiet.

"Well?" She studied his face with worry.

"There is certainly a shard of glass."

"Then kindly remove it."

She tried to look over her shoulder and saw only blood running down her arm. How had she not noticed?

He was already searching through the small cottage for something to stop the blood. He found a napkin in the food hamper and applied it as gingerly as he could.

"Why couldn't I have paid more attention to Elly? She loves this kind of thing. I'm not overly fond of blood myself. I can't see a deuced thing in this light and the flow won't stop."

"Here, let me hold it. I'll apply pressure. See if you can gather some water to wash it, and then perhaps you may be able to see the glass better."

"Yes, I remember that's what they said to do in the Army. Don't think we need a tourniquet yet."

"A tourniquet? I should hope not! For a shard of glass?"

He looked at her shoulder unconvincingly.

She could almost laugh at the absurdity.

He returned with a few small pieces of linen. He wet one and began to wash her shoulder.

"I am not certain how to remove this."

"You do not think you could pull it out with your fingers?" she asked.

"I'm not certain. I will try, but I am afraid to do more damage. There are no proper tools for this sort of thing here."

"Try, and if you cannot, then we will try to stop the blood until we return." If she could reach she would try herself. "You will not hurt me. Go on," she said reassuringly.

He took hold of the glass and pulled.

She was determined not to move or cry. But it hurt badly. Much worse than it had before, and worse than anything she had ever felt before. It was difficult to breathe.

"Are you all right?"

She nodded through gritted teeth. "Is it still bleeding?"

"Yes. I will need to pack it with any linen we can find and we will half to wrap it as tight as we can."

"We can tear strips from the bottom of my petticoat."

Once the bleeding was controlled, she looked around curiously for the offending shard while Mr Abbott flung himself exhaustedly across the bed.

"Where is the piece of glass you removed?"

"I do not think that is a good idea for you to see it."

She wanted to know how a little piece of glass had hurt so bloody badly.

"I wish to see it." He raised his head up and looked at her sceptically, then walked over to the table where he had placed it. He handed it to her and she gasped.

"Dear me! I was wondering what the fuss was about. I confess I thought I was mistaken in your experience on the battlefield."

In her hand was a rather large piece of glass that looked like an icicle.

"If this had hit a few inches in the other direction I would be dead."

"I realise that. Now you might understand why I was terrified. I did not know how deep the glass was embedded. I've enough battlefield experience to be afraid."

"Now you understand how I felt watching you try to cross the bridge." He eyed her thoughtfully.

"Indeed. I was less frightened in the river than I was just now."

"Mr Abbott, I am dreadfully sorry I put you in this position. You should have left me here."

"You should know I could never do such a thing."

He came over and knelt before her. He took her hands and looked into her eyes for a few moments thoughtfully.

"I would rather be here with you than anywhere else." Her heart stuttered at the quiet intensity in his voice. He stood up and kissed the top of her head, and walked over to the bed as if not wanting to see her reaction.

She felt empty as he walked away, and she longed to call him back to her. His words pierced her heart, and she was more confused than ever before. She snuggled down into the sofa, ignoring the pain that was now shooting down her arm, and prayed for the rain to slow and her emotions to calm.

She must have fallen asleep, for she woke disoriented, and her foot hanging over the side was...wet. She sat up and looked about as a small amount of daylight crept into the room. Did this mean that the rain had stopped, or had the river flooded into the cottage? The water level was currently at the bottom of the sofa cushion. She looked over to the bed where Mr Abbott was sleeping blissfully unaware.

Chapter Eighteen

"Mr Abbott!"

Andrew resisted waking from a heavenly dream where Gwen and he were trapped in the summer house. He rolled over on a tiny bed he did not recognise.

"Mr Abbott!"

Perhaps it wasn't a dream, for the voice calling his name seemed near. He popped one eye open and surveyed his surroundings, as was his custom from his time in the army. A habit he could not break. He came upon his Titian- headed goddess wrapped in a toga with her red locks dishevelled about her, standing on the sofa. Maybe it was a dream after all. He smiled and closed his eye willing his dream to completion.

"Andrew, please wake up!"

That was definitely her voice shouting, and she was definitely in the room with him. He sat up clutching his blanket, recalling his wits enough for modesty.

"Good morning, beautiful." He smiled sleepily.

"Good morning," she said as if she were greeting him for tea. "Would you be so obliging as to fetch my clothes before they become damp again?"

He suddenly recalled why they were there and looked down to see the floodwaters rising towards him.

"Certainly." He lifted his 'skirts' and trudged gingerly towards the fireplace where the clothes had been hung.

The bottoms of her skirts and his pantaloons were already wet, but they would be better than attempting to wear a blanket while swimming. He had upended his boots on the bedposts and sighed at their sad state: he would be making no society appearances for some time at least. He handed Miss Lambert her clothes and climbed up on the bed to don his.

He turned away from her. "No peeking, Miss Lambert."

"I would not dream of it."

"I believe I've been properly set down!" he said appreciatively.

"Is that possible?" she retorted amiably.

He smiled and was tempted beyond measure to turn and peek if only to tease her. He had no doubt she was even dressing with propriety by trying to hide under the blanket.

"Do you need help? What is taking so long?" It took all of his restraint not to go help as he heard her struggling.

"I don't fancy you have ever attempted to put on women's clothing. Nor have done it one-handedly."

"Well, there was this one time at Eton...no, perhaps that story is best left unspoken. Do you need my help?"

"Need it? Yes. Want it..." her voice trailed away.

"Miss Lambert, I'm turning around," he warned.

He turned around to find her with a face that was extremely pale and watching blood stream down her arm.

He immediately rushed over and picked her up and took her to the bed, wading through water up to his knees. He tore what remained of her petticoat and began applying pressure to her wound. He looked around the cottage, and hoped the water would cease rising. They would soon be on the roof, and he did not know how he would manage that feat with her weak and bleeding.

"Is it stopped?"

"I think it is slowing."

"I must have aggravated it attempting to dress. I managed one arm at least."

"You did shockingly well. I am going to tie this tight, and then attempt to save the food and see if any of the boats survived the storm."

"Boats?"

"Only small row boats we keep for fishing and recreation, but it would be better than drowning."

He took the hamper of food and hung it on the hook by the door, and brought her a chunk of bread and an apple from it.

"You best eat. You are losing strength as it is, and I am not certain how long we will be stranded here. If I cannot find a boat, we will be obliged to climb to the roof or hope the table floats."

Andrew had difficulty opening the door due to the water pressure. Once the door was opened, he understood the old adage about floodgates. He could see the water flowing rapidly outside, but the skies were clearing. He had very little practical knowledge about rivers and flooding, he acknowledged to himself. He looked around at the fallen trees and the swollen river and had no idea how long it would take to recede. He had never seen anything like it.

He hoped the manor house was high enough to evade the waters, but he could not worry over that when he needed to get Miss Lambert to safety.

He made his way around the cottage holding on to the sides of the structure, hoping the boats were not all set adrift in the storm. The river currents looked too dangerous to cross, and he had no desire to be swept away to explore America at the moment. The larger boats were nowhere to be seen, but a small rowboat hung on a hook on the wall. He shook his head at the oddity of the small boat being the one that had survived, but was thankful nevertheless. He pulled the boat down and guided it by its rope as he made his way to the front of the cottage looking for a safe place to tie it and wait out the worst of the flood.

~*~

She could only stare at him out of the door as he splashed through the water. She hoped he returned quickly, because she did not know how to swim.

It felt like an eternity since he had left her. She eyed the water warily as it crept towards her. She would soon be obliged to cling to the bedposts, and she needed to use the necessary. How she was to manage that awkward order of business in the midst of a flood or stranded on a boat, she could not imagine.

When Mr Abbott at last returned, she was willing herself to calm down. "Thank God!"

"Did you think I left you after going through all this trouble in the first place?"

"Of course not, but I need to...to..."

How could she put it politely?

Understanding crossed his face. "Oh. Why didn't you say so?"

"You weren't here, and one does not normally speak of such things," she said exasperated.

"You could walk, the water is not so deep."

"I did not know where to go and I can't swim!" she said in a slight panic.

"I don't know where you'll go either," he said most helpfully. "I suppose...no, that won't do." He pondered as she stood watching him in horror, fearing she would be obliged to embarrass herself beyond belief.

"I've got it." He held up his finger proudly. He splashed through the now waist-high water and picked her up carefully.

"How's the shoulder?"

"Better I think, as long as I don't move it."

He carried her outside staying on the porch around to a small ledge and set her down on it.

"I'll just go around the corner and you say when you are finished."

She looked around her in disbelief. "You expect me to go here?"

"It is the best I can do." He shrugged. "You get used to using Nature in the Army."

"I am not in the Army, and I cannot just go like a man! Forgive my indelicacy, but I did have a brother, and our bodies are rather different, if you recall," she said with her face flushing beet red.

"I cannot believe I am having this conversation." He was blushing now.

"Trust me, nothing could have prepared me for this moment," she murmured.

He cleared his throat. "Your only other option is to jump into the water. I will let you choose." With that helpful array of choices, he turned and escaped around the corner.

She took a deep breath. She would never be able to look him in the eye again. She only thought she had been humiliated before. It seemed as if the entire forest was watching and listening. She looked around at this small ledge and decided to try her ingenuity and pray he could not hear as she hummed nervously. She was too miserable not to.

When she decided to overcome her mortification in favour of departing the ledge, she finally called out to him.

"See now. It isn't so terrible being at one with Nature," he said as he scooped her into his arms.

"May we not speak on Nature? I am not terribly fond of her at the moment. I'm certain that years later I will laugh about it, but I would rather be safe in England and forget all of this."

"If only it did not require journeying by ship."

He carried her to the small boat he had tied to the post in front of the house and placed her inside. He had fetched the hamper of food, the blankets he could salvage, and her bonnet inside for her and climbed in across from her.

"So we row back to the house?"

"No. We wait."

"We wait?" she wanted to scream.

"The creek is flowing too fast to cross. We would be swept away."

"How long will we be in this boat?"

"I've no idea. If it doesn't rain anymore, perhaps only a day or two. If we are really fortunate, the men might be able to come for us in a larger boat if they have enough strength to fight the current."

"Why are the waters still rising since the rain stopped?"

"I suppose it has something to do with the tides as we are near the ocean. In the meantime, we have each other's delightful company."

"Indeed." She put her hands to her face and winced from the pain in her shoulder.

"What were you doing here anyway?"

"Painting." She had forgotten about the painting. "My painting! I suppose it is lost."

"No, I will go after it. If the dashed thing was important enough to risk your pretty neck in the storm, I will see if it is salvageable."

"It was on the mantle."

"There might be hope for it there."

The poor man slipped over the side of the bobbing boat into the water

231

as she held on for dear life. He returned shortly holding the beloved canvas above his head.

"If nothing else, it will provide shade," he remarked as he placed it in the boat and climbed in.

She cast an annoyed look at him and he grinned unabashedly at her.

"You are ever cheerful in a dire situation."

"Might as well make the best of it."

"I suppose the Army was worse than this. I would be best to cease waxing on about our plight."

"You may wax on about anything you like."

"Perhaps later. I am feeling a trifle fatigued. I would give anything for a dry bed at the moment."

"We will have to make do with a dry boat."

She cast him an unappreciative glance.

"I meant nothing improper whatsoever. However, if you wish to lie down, I can swim for a while."

"That will not be necessary. I appreciate the sacrifice. Besides, who will keep my painting dry?" she parried.

"I have my uses. Lean this way and I will attempt to make a pillow from the blankets."

They gingerly arranged themselves in the tiny boat, but she was too fatigued to argue when he placed her head to rest on his shoulder. He had placed the painting at an angle so as to shield them from the sun, and the roar of the water and the rocking of the boat lulled them both to sleep.

Gwen awoke some time later to her sleeping limbs intertwined with his. She was startled to the point of nearly overturning them in the small vessel.

"Hush, my lamb. It will be all right."

She looked around and instantly recalled their situation, wondering how long she had slept, and how much longer they would be obliged to remain in this tiny conveyance. Were the situation different between them, she might not have minded being stranded with him. Neither of them had any inclination to discuss the future after last night's proceedings, for the moment grateful that they had survived thus far. They fell back into easy banter, trying to while away the boredom.

"What shall we do to pass the time? Do you fancy any naming games or fishing?" he suggested.

"And how would you propose we catch the fish?"

"Oh, ye of little faith!" he said, offended.

"Feel free to amuse yourself—and me—while you make the attempt," she taunted.

"I'm not certain what I should do with a fish if I should catch it."

"For myself, I'm perfectly content to never see another fish."

"All this talk of food is making me hungry. Is there anything left in the hamper?"

"I cannot bear the thought of eating." She did not care to have any more mortifying episodes.

"You need to eat to maintain your strength," he insisted.

"I will when I must," she maintained.

"A soldier learns to eat when he can," he argued.

"One would think a wise soldier would learn to ration," she sallied, though quietly.

"Food rots."

"You win. I am too tired to care."

She conceded to a small sip of wine and a biscuit and put her head back down on his shoulder.

Thus the pair was rescued, arguing as brother and sister, two days after Gwen had set out in her fit of pique. And though it had been bliss to be in Mr Abbott's presence, and he had uttered no words of reproach, it only made the realisation that she was not fit to be his wife all the more poignant. A proper lady would have known to remain in England; a proper lady would not have not made rash decisions or put so many in jeopardy by venturing out in a storm.

Perhaps she had wronged him and he did not seek the attentions of the scheming Bradley chit. Either way, he deserved someone more fitted to the task of being his lady. When they heard the first call to them from their rescuers, Gwen was by that time so weak that she could only greet them with a faint smile and wet eyes; Mr Abbott was more urgent in his demands, shouting for them to hurry, that she needed a doctor. Gwen did not think she needed anything of the sort, and also thought it unlikely a doctor able to come to her aid at any rate in the floods.

She was lifted into a larger boat and swiftly back into Mr Abbott's arms.

"What happened to her?" Nathaniel asked with concern.

"A large piece of glass lodged into her shoulder when a tree shot through the window. She lost a fair amount of blood."

"Let us move quickly then." The men began to row swiftly at his signal.

"How bad is the damage at the house?" Andrew asked.

"Not as bad as I thought it would be at the start. The river overflowed into the house during the worst of the storm, but it is on higher ground than the summer house and has receded. Your quick thinking servants were able to save most of the food and have already begun putting the house back into order."

"I gather the fields are a complete loss?"

"We have not gone to look. Our first thought was to find you."

"Much obliged to you."

As they rowed against the still raging currents of the river, they passed many barely visible roofs of the servants' cottages. It would be some time before they recovered from this sizable storm. No one remarked on the obvious, but a solemn silence remained until they arrived upon the ground surrounding the house.

~*~

Gwen was tired and ached all over. She struggled to wake up from her semi-conscious state. She was aware of someone holding her hand and stroking her hair, but it was too much effort to open her eyes.

"Is she finally waking up?" a familiar voice asked.

"She has stirred a little," Andrew replied.

"Poor thing. She is done worn out. Have you been getting her to drink?" Josie asked.

"Very little."

"Don't you worry, Master Andrew. She will perk up soon."

Gwen began to assimilate her surroundings and recall the previous day's events: the storm and the boat. She was finally able to open her eyes and looked towards Andrew who was sitting next to her.

"Good afternoon," he said with a relieved smile.

"Afternoon?" she tried to speak, but her mouth was dry.

He instantly got up to give her a drink. "You must be parched. You have scarcely had anything to eat or drink in two days."

When her thirst was quenched, she asked, "How long have I been asleep?"

"An entire day."

She sat up and flinched with pain in her shoulder and remembered the injury. That must account for her unusual fatigue.

"Does your shoulder pain you?"

"A little. I had forgotten and was not careful."

"Josie does not think it serious. She thinks it will heal without issue."

Gwen nodded and an awkward silence fell. So much had happened in the past two days she did not know where to begin.

"We need to speak, Gwen. I know you are tired, but we must resolve some things between us."

"I don't know what to say or what to think anymore."

"Why won't you just let me take care of you? Am I mistaken in your feelings for me?"

"No," she said quietly looking down at her hands. "But I do not think I could not live with my conscience. I still have a shred of dignity remaining."

"I see. Marriage to me would be so distasteful?"

"Marriage?" she looked up with surprise.

"What did you think I was offering?" Suddenly so much made sense. "You thought…"

"You never said the word," she protested. "I had convinced myself it was an honourable offer, and then when I arrived I convinced myself it couldn't be. You would be lowering yourself when you could have any of these wealthy ladies fawning over you."

"Please do not be ridiculous or insulting!"

"And how was I to know if you were offering *carte blanche* or marriage?"

"You should know nothing of that!"

"I have been offered it more times than I would care to remember. I know precisely what it is!"

"But I never!" he exclaimed.

"You never said the word," she explained. "I allowed myself to be convinced by your sister and mislaid my mind somewhere between Somerset and Sussex! Between losing my mother, my home and being lied to and compromised by my cousin."

"Attempt to compromise," he corrected.

"Yes, yes." She waved away his interruption. "I believe I might say under the circumstances, it is difficult to see clearly. Perhaps my mother's madness is beginning to affect me too." Her eyes grew wide as she had not before considered her mother's madness might pass to her. "See! I am not fit to be anybody's wife *or mistress*."

"My delusional, impossible, adorable Gwen." He sat on the bed next to her and held her hands. "You are driving *me* to madness. Can you not see that none of your objections matter to me? That you and I were meant to be? There is no other woman for me. I do apologise for Miss Bradley, and I promise I will do my best to make it clear to any woman who endeavours to come within five feet of me in the future."

Her eyes were filling with tears. Silence. And more silence. He couldn't even read her face. She was staring off into the distance with no emotion whatsoever. That could not be good. He made a note to mention to her a future in cards if she turned him down. Maybe his proposal wasn't romantic enough.

"You must say yes. I did truly compromise you. We were alone for two days. My reputation will not survive if you refuse me."

She was staring at her hands.

"Very well. You have forced me to take drastic measures." He picked her up and carried her out of the room.

"Andrew! What are you doing? Put me down!"

He ignored her protests, carrying her down the stairs to where most everyone from the estate was involved in cleaning the aftereffects of the flood.

"May I have your attention?" he shouted.

He found a chair and set her gingerly upon it.

The servants and children gathered around. Lord and Lady Fairmont came into the room to see what the commotion was about. When he had everyone's attention he dropped to one knee before her and took her hand. She began to tremble with nervousness and felt self-conscious as everyone in the room watched.

"It seems I have made a complete mull of my good intentions, dearest Gwen." He stared into her eyes as he spoke. "From the moment I saw you, I was intrigued. From the time we spent together, I was enchanted. From now until forever, I am captivated. Please say you will be mine. I do not wish to live another day without you by my side. Will you marry me?"

He pulled out a beautiful ruby ring and placed it on her finger. She swallowed nervously, and everyone in the room held their breath. She nodded as tears streamed down her face, and threw her arms around him.

"A virtuous woman I have found: your worth is far above rubies, and I will cherish you until my dying breath, Gwen."

"I thought you would never ask, Uncle Andrew," Amelia said with relief, and to the amusement of the crowd.

"Nathaniel, would you please send for the Reverend?" Andrew begged.

"So soon?" Gwen asked.

"Yes!" Andrew answered.

"We should see to clearing up first," Gwen said as she looked around.

"Can we not find the Reverend first?" he pleaded.

"Certainly, if you would be so good as to row the boat," Nathaniel remarked to no one, observing the flooded land out of the window.

"I think we should wait until the rest of your family can be with us," Gwen reasoned.

"They will be happy enough to see me riveted. They will not mind overmuch," Andrew said reassuringly.

"I would like them to be present. I have no family of my own left, and your family is very close."

"No, I will not wait one more day. We are here for who knows how long, and I have no intention of remaining a gentleman for an entire Atlantic crossing."

"I am not concerned. We will both be spending most of the time green and bent over the side rails."

"No, I will not set foot on the boat unless you are Mrs Abbott."

"Then I suggest we begin cleaning."

"You are going back to bed. I made my point and you must rest," he said with authority.

Oblivious to her protests, he scooped her up and carried her back to her room.

Chapter Nineteen

One month later…

"Please, Gwen. I am only human," Andrew pleaded.

"We may leave in two weeks, Andrew."

Bang!

"By Jove, you hit it!" Andrew exclaimed. "Capital shot!"

Gwen did not share her betrothed's delight. "Why must we shoot rabbits again?"

"We need them for food," he said patiently, though he had explained this every time she had shot something.

Gwen could not deny the food was needed. Prices were beyond all but the richest men's purses, but even a rich man could not buy when there was none to be had. The flooding left by the storm had devastated farms to the Shenandoah Valley. Her brother had taught her to shoot, but she did not enjoy killing anything. She had volunteered because she knew her skill would be useful, but she did not like it. Shooting had been much more enjoyable when it was wafers or a target she was aiming at.

"Cheer up, my lamb. You will not be obliged to hunt for your food much longer."

She nodded and turned her head away as the dogs brought back the evidence of her success.

"You have allowed several men to be useful repairing the house and the fields, instead of having to hunt. As soon as we celebrate the Thanksgiving feast, we will depart."

"There is much to be thankful for," Gwen remarked. The storm had devastated the servants' cottages and severely damaged the fields. They had worked long days and some nights to make the cottages habitable and get the fields repaired and replanted in time for spring.

"Now to find some turkeys. I know they are around. They were spotted several times this week near the pond in the woodland."

"Then let us find them," she said, resigned.

"You have more mettle than I bargained for, my love. I am, in fact, the luckiest man alive," he looked at her appreciatively.

"Gwen," he said her name in a throaty voice that made her knees weak. She was trapped in his gaze. He took her face in his hands and bent his head to hers. His lips were gentle but firm, insistent yet caressing. Her heart's emptiness was filled with something she could not describe. She had only known something was missing. She wrapped her arms around his neck and dared to kiss him back as his fingers combed through her hair.

"It looks like we arrived in the nick of time," the Dowager's voice said sardonically.

"I never thought I would be so excited to hear your voice, Gran." Andrew smiled and placed one more kiss on his beloved's lips before turning to his grandmother.

"Rapscallion!" the Dowager retorted with relish. She had missed her sparring partner.

Gwen was flushing to her roots, but she was enormously pleased to see the Dowager.

Andrew opened his arms to welcome his grandmother, who decided to abandon all sense of propriety and embrace them both.

"Thank God you came. Gwen insisted we wait to marry until we could have the family present."

"I had little choice in the matter. When your sister got wind of things, she decided to give birth and set sail."

"Elly is here?" Gwen gasped.

"Not even Easton could keep that headstrong girl from boarding the ship. She would not be kept away."

"That's Elly. Pluck to the backbone!" Andrew remarked fondly.

"Or over-plucked," the Dowager muttered. She eyed a rifle in Gwen's hand and gave Andrew a scathing look. "Are you making her earn her keep? There are more genteel ways for ladies to be occupied my dear."

"I volunteered," Gwen said with becoming meekness.

"She is a better shot than any of the men. We needed her talents to feed the lot of them after the storm."

"Indeed." The Dowager looked at the carcasses with distaste. "Well, shall we venture back to the house? You may wash, then meet your new niece."

"You mean to tell me Elly brought the baby?" Gwen asked with dismay.

"And the triplets." The Dowager nodded as if she concurred with the insanity of the decision. "She insisted they needed to become acquainted with River's Bend. She would not be parted from them for so long. I am decidedly too old for these modern notions."

"Ignore her, Gwen. Elly is the spitting image of Gran. She was famous for the larks she kicked up in her day."

"You may go ahead." The Dowager shooed him and the string of rabbits away. "Gwen is capable of walking me back to the house."

"As you wish, ma'am." He bowed and walked away with a roguish smile.

Gwen lovingly watched him leave.

"Are you very tired, ma'am?" she asked as she and the Dowager strolled.

"Not a bit. I think sea travel agrees with me. I might head to Italy and the Greek Isles from here. I've always wanted to see them, but never thought I cared for seafaring. I suppose one is never too old to try something new."

"No, indeed." Gwen's eyes twinkled.

"Now, dearest, tell me why you insisted on waiting to marry that handsome grandson of mine. If it had been me, I would have held that shotgun at his back and marched him down the aisle at the first opportunity."

"It did not seem proper to not have you here. And, the plantation was devastated. I know you cannot tell by looking now, but the entire place was under water. It would not have been right to have insisted on my happiness at that moment."

"Very well, suit yourself. I, on the other hand, would not have had the self-restraint. Perhaps I am biased."

Gwen choked on her laughter.

The Dowager's eyes crinkled and she cast a sideways glance at her. "Well, now that Easton, Elly and Sir Charles are here, we may see you married and leave the rest in their hands. Because I have a notion to winter in Italy and Greece, I need some escorts. She leaned in closer and whispered even though there was no one around, "I sleep very soundly." She winked at Gwen and hurried into the house, leaving Gwen staring after her in astonishment.

Andrew had already found his niece and was cuddling her to him. If Gwen had held any doubts, at that moment a maternal urge stirred and silenced them forever. She watched in adoration and did not notice Lord and Lady Easton standing beside her.

"Adam, you'd best send for Reverend Norris. Abe can escort you," Elly said knowingly, as she caught Gwen watching Andrew.

"Yes, dear. But first, Miss Lambert, would you mind if we spoke in private?"

She looked surprised, but said, "Not at all. I believe the study would be quiet." She led him into the room and closed the door.

"I apologise for seeming strange, but I felt it best to inform you of what I found before you proceeded."

She sat and waved for him to do the same.

"Do you recall that I inquired of the Kendall's solicitor before you left?"

"Vaguely. I confess I had all but forgotten."

He nodded. "There was much to be desired in the way Kendall dealt with you." He handed her a letter. "We decided it would be best for him to explain the circumstances to you himself."

She took the letter sceptically and opened it. She began to read the lines in disbelief.

"He humbly begs my pardon," she read aloud with a gasp. "Very civil of him." She had no doubt what had led him to apologise.

"He says my grandfather left a marriage portion to me in his will."

She muttered through a few more lines, "His father attempted to have it overturned. I do not doubt for a moment," she said with distaste. "You did teach him a proper lesson, did you not?"

He nodded. "With pleasure. He will be fortunate to produce heirs in the future."

She looked satisfied and went back to the letter. "If we had married each other, the entire fortune would have been his. That explains much."

She continued, "If I married another, I would receive half."

She dropped the letter into her lap. "I suppose greediness overcame good sense."

"Perhaps." Easton remarked, amused. "Did you read to the end?"

She looked back to the paper and saw the amount. Her eyes grew wide. "Greediness indeed!"

"Miss Lambert, you are a wealthy woman. And you will not have to worry about Kendall again."

"Only if I marry."

"What do you mean *if* you marry?" Andrew demanded, as he entered the room still holding baby Henrietta.

Easton stood with a smile on his face and walked over to take his precious bundle from Andrew. "I believe I will see to the good Reverend now."

"You have some explaining to do."

She pulled his face down to hers. "After we're married."

"You do not have to tell me twice."

He made do with the nonverbal explanation for now.

Chapter Twenty

One year later…

"Well, my dear, does it fulfill your expectations?" Andrew asked as he put his arms around his wife from behind.

Gwen looked out over the crystal blue waters from their terrace. "It is beyond what I'd imagined. I cannot wait to paint it."

"Paint as much as you like. When you fill every wall, I will build more walls," he murmured, while continuing to shower his beloved with gentle kisses.

"How long will we be here?"

"Until I surprise you with somewhere new."

Gwen could not help but smile. This was the third country they'd visited since they had left America.

"Will we ever return home?"

Andrew stopped his attentions abruptly. "Do you want to go home?"

"Perhaps one day."

"I am here to fulfill your heart's desire." He smiled rakishly down at her.

Gwen blushed, even after nearly a year of being married.

"I know." She stopped to bestow a handsome kiss on her love. If someone had told her two years ago how her life would have changed for the better, she would not have believed it possible. "I do wish to see your family again. To have our children know their family."

"Are you trying to tell me something?"

"No. Not yet." Gwen subconsciously touched her stomach. She had thought she would be with child by this point. She refused to feel disappointed. She was blessed beyond measure. If she could not have her own, she would be the best aunt to Elly and Sarah's children she could. Or maybe they could adopt some orphans. Perhaps she was too old for her own.

"Why the glum face?" Andrew asked with a furrowed brow. "Because I will do anything in my power to erase it."

She shook off her reverie and smiled lovingly at him. "I think returning to England after we have had our fill of Italy would be nice. We do not have to see the entire world in one trip."

Andrew looked at her with guilt.

"What is it?"

"I might have promised the family we would meet them in France for Christmas."

"Will everyone be there?"

He nodded, "Everyone," he said emphatically. "The *entire* Loring-Abbott clan."

She smiled. "That will be lovely. I look forward to it." And she would. She had longed for a large, loving family. Hers had never been such, even before they'd been isolated by her father's disgrace.

"You do realise that includes the Duke and Duchess, Nathaniel, Lydia, Amelia, Robert, Easton, Elly, Charlie, Gary, Lizzy, Hettie, Vernon, Beatrice, Olivia, and Ben?" He inhaled after rattling off the list. "I'm exhausted thinking on it."

She laughed. "Afraid of your nieces and nephews?"

"Absolutely!" He looked at her as if she were daft.

"You brought it upon yourself."

He eyed her with mock disdain.

She wrinkled her face. "You did not mention your grandmother. Does she mean to stay here?"

He shrugged. "I've no idea. She hasn't said."

"You do not think..." her voice trailed off.

"Who can say? I have never seen her act like such a ninny around a man."

"The Count is lovely. I would think you would be happy for her, Andrew. No matter your age, everyone deserves love."

"Do you think it love? I never considered it. Nor do I wish to." He shook his face with mock repulsion.

She swatted at him.

"I had better look into this count more closely tomorrow."

"I think she can take care of herself."

"I would have thought so too, until I saw how she was behaving around him."

"Oh, Andrew."

"Do not deprive me of this chance to meddle with my grandmother." He began nibbling on her ear.

"Let us not talk anymore about them. I want to behave like a ninny with you."

He began to loosen her tapes, and all thoughts of the Dowager were gone.

Thank you for reading *Shadows of Doubt*! I hope you enjoyed it. If you did, please help other readers find this book:

1. This ebook is lendable, so send it to a friend who you think might like it so she or he can discover me, too.

2. Help other people find this book by writing a review.

3. Sign up for my new releases at www.Elizabethjohnsauthor.com, so you can find out about the next book as soon as it's available.

4. Come like my Facebook page www.facebook.com/Elizabethjohnsauthor or follow on Twitter @Ejohnsauthor or feel free to write me at elizabethjohnsauthor@gmail.com

Other Titles by Elizabeth Johns:

Surrender the Past

Seasons of Change

Seeking Redemption

Second Dance

Through the Fire

About the Author

Like many writers, Elizabeth Johns was first an avid reader, though she was a reluctant convert. It was Jane Austen's clever wit and unique turn of phrase that hooked Johns when she was 'forced' to read Pride and Prejudice for a school assignment. She began writing when she ran out of her favourite author's books and decided to try her hand at crafting a Regency romance novel. Her journey into publishing began with the release of Surrender the Past, book one of the Loring-Abbott Series. Johns makes no pretensions to Austen's wit, but hopes readers will perhaps laugh and find some enjoyment in her writing.

Johns attributes much of her inspiration to her mother, a former English teacher. During their last summer together, Johns would sit on the porch swing and read her stories to her mother, who encouraged her to continue writing. Busy with multiple careers, including a professional job in the medical field, writing and mother of small children, Johns squeezes in time for reading whenever possible.

Preview of Through the Fire ...

Gavin looked at the letter in his hand in utter disbelief. His heart was tearing in two. His brother, wife, and children had been killed when their carriage had slipped down the side of a cliff.

"This canna be true." He shook his head and fought back tears.

"I'm afraid it is, my lord."

"My lord? No. I doona wish for it. I'm a simple country doctor. I have a humble life and practice here."

"I'm terribly sorry for your loss, my lord. But you are, in fact, the eleventh Baron Craig now, and thus have some rather large holdings that are your responsibility."

"This was not supposed to happen. Iain had three strapping young lads!"

The solicitor looked grave. "Perhaps, my lord, it would be best for you to return to Castle Craig and see for yourself."

The solicitor was met with a blank stare from a set of startling blue eyes; a look that was common to those who had been met with grievous news, but who had not yet assimilated the ensuing change in circumstances.

"Verra well. I'll join you there as soon as I have made arrangements."

Gavin went through the motions of closing up his house and seeing his practice into the capable hands of his apprentice from Lord Easton's school. He had taken many trips to England to the school in Sussex of late and had toyed with joining it as an instructor full time, but he had never been able to cut ties with Scotland. How would he practice medicine as Lord Craig? He would have to find a way, but he would also do his best to carry on with his brother's works in Parliament.

Gavin had seen more death than most, but he had not been prepared for the loss of his brother, or of Iain's wife and children. They had been the last family he'd had left. He'd never given a thought to running the large Castle Craig estate, and hoped desperately that his brother had appointed a trustworthy steward.

His carriage was loaded with immediate necessities. His servants would send the rest of his belongings with those of his staff who wished to join him at the new residence. He had one final stop before setting off to bury his brother and begin his new life.

He pulled through the gates of Alberfoyle Priory, one of Lord Vernon's estates that served as an orphanage. He had become attached to a family of children there; the boy was attending medical school, but the two girls were still in residence. It would pain him to leave these children more than anything else. In fact, since he had no family of his own, perhaps they would consider allowing him to adopt them.

"Dr Craig!" Maili Douglas came running when she saw him and greeted him with a hug. She was promptly lifted off her feet into his arms.

"Hello, my love. Where is your sister?"

"In the sewing class."

"Would you be so good as to retrieve her? I would like to speak to you both."

The little girl wrinkled her forehead in concern, but then nodded and skipped off to find her sister. She returned with Catriona, who received the same welcome as her sister had.

"Hello, lass. You have grown again!"

"Am I not supposed to grow?"

"Indeed you are. Only not too fast." Gavin choked up as he thought of his three nephews who he would never see again, and who would never grow any older...

"Why are you sad, Dr Craig?" Maili asked.

"I found out that my brother and his family have died."

"Like our mama and papa?" Catriona cocked her head up to look at him.

"Yes, lass. Just like that."

Catriona and Maili crawled into his lap to comfort him. "Are you all alone like us now?"

"I am, and that is part of what I wanted to speak to you about. I have to move away, and would not be able to see you as often."

"Please don't leave us!" the girls cried.

"I was hoping you would come with me—and Seamus, too, when he is home from school. Would you like that?"

"Would you be our new papa?" Catriona asked.

"I would adopt you, yes. But I will never try to replace your papa or mama."

The girls threw their arms around his neck.

"That would be perfect."

"I will return for you after I have arranged everything with your guardian and buried my brother."

"Must you leave us?"

"I am afraid so, but I will be back for you soon." He exchanged hugs with the girls and took his leave to go and bury his brother and his family.

~*~

Lady Margaux Ashbury had wanted to join a convent, but her parents had insisted she instead remove to their new orphanage north of Glasgow for a short repairing lease before doing something so drastic. She had been enamoured with Scotland when she had visited Lord Vernon's estate while they were courting a few years back. Despite her less fortunate outcome, she still loved Scotland.

After Lord Vernon had married his true love instead, her family had attempted to divert her with trips to London and to the Continent after Napoleon was defeated. But she had come to the realisation that she was content on her own. She had always been the most independent of her sisters, and decided that brilliant marriages could be left in their capable hands. She certainly preferred the spinster state to marrying for convenience. She found she was content helping with the orphans, though she did very little with the establishment's competent staff which her family had appointed.

"What are you pondering, *mon amie*?" Margaux heard her

mother ask.

"Very little, *Maman*," she remarked, as they sat darning socks for some of the children. Her parents had remained with her, hopeful to change her mind.

"We are having a guest for dinner tonight. Someone interested in contributing to the orphans."

"*Tres bien*," she said absentmindedly. Guests were a normal occurrence with her parents.

"You should wear the emerald satin. Bring some colour to your face, *non?*"

"If you wish, *Maman*." Margaux cared little for what she wore these days.

"*Allons y*." Lady Ashbury stood and directed her daughter to do the same. "I will see you at dinner."

Lady Margaux went through the motions of dressing. Her maid arranged her hair in a manner worthy of a ball, she noticed. She must admit she had been having a mild case of the dismals. Once she established a routine here she would come out of it, she was certain. She had never been one to sulk, but she needed to find something useful to occupy her time. No, she corrected her thoughts. To make a new life.

She made her way downstairs, determined to be more cheerful. If she could only convince her parents she was happy here, then they would be satisfied she was content.

"Ah, there she is now, Lord Craig," Lord Ashbury remarked.

"Dr Craig?" Margaux said, stunned as she met the eyes of the handsome doctor who had been enamoured of Lady Beatrice.

Made in the USA
Middletown, DE
25 May 2016